GHOSTS OF THE
TRISTAN BASIN

September 2nd,
2018

GHOSTS OF THE
TRISTAN BASIN

BRIAN MCCLELLAN

Typesetting and ebook conversion by handebooks.co.uk.

E*ight months before the events of* Promise of Blood...

Tristan Basin

To Redstone

Planth

Stillwater

Major Buter's Camp

Gladeside

Basin Highway

To Landfall

N
W E
S

Taniel Two-shot crept through the murky, chest-deep water of the Tristan Basin, eyes scanning the surface for the tell-tale ripple of boas and swamp dragons. He clung to the shadows of the big cypress trees, his rifle, kit, and powder horn held over his head. The sounds of the droning insects, bird calls, and the occasional *splunk* of an animal slipping into the water were drown out by the heavy thumping of his own heart, echoing in his ears like a kettle drum.

Despite his reservations about the local wildlife—it was not unheard of for the unwary to be pulled beneath the water, never to resurface—Taniel had more immediate concerns. There were eighty Kez soldiers nearby, if his Palo guides were to be believed, each of them armed with the very best muskets and accompanied by local guides of their own.

One of them stood on a dry hummock of land not twenty paces away from Taniel's position, his back toward the water.

Taniel's toe caught an exposed root and he felt his heart leap into his throat as he drifted forward, chin dipping dangerously into the water. He resisted the urge to gulp loudly for air and instead pushed off with his other foot, keeping his head and rifle above the surface. The movement caused a slight disturbance against the base of the nearest cypress.

Up ahead, the Kez soldier gave no indication he'd noticed.

Taniel paused and held his breath as the ripples subsided, then continued forward. The bank rose sharply, and Taniel's bare shoulders, then chest, then the belt of his buckskins emerged from the water. He set his rifle and equipment on the bank of the hummock, drawing his belt knife.

It took him three strides before he was on top of the Kez guard, snaking one hand around to cover the man's mouth and pressing the blade of the knife to his throat with the other.

"One sound and you're dead," Taniel whispered in Kez. "Nod if you understand."

The soldier stiffened at the touch of the knife. This close, Taniel could smell the sweat and fungal rot of his skin, and the lingering odor of shit from a case of dysentery. The soldier was probably in his mid-twenties—older than Taniel by at least five years—with large, black sideburns and a fresh scar on the side of his chin. He gave a slight, trembling nod.

"Good," Taniel said. "My name's Captain Taniel Two-shot, and I'm running a pretty heavy powder trance right now. I could kill you but I'd rather not, so let's do this easy, all right?" He removed his hand from the soldier's mouth. "What's your name?"

"Private Jibble, sir."

Taniel took the powder charges from Jibble's kit and tucked them into Jibble's jacket pocket, patting them gently then disarmed him. He fetched his own kit and rifle and returned to the soldier's side.

Jibble stood stiff as a board. A slight tremor in his voice betrayed his fear. "You're the powder mage?" he asked in a whisper. "The one who killed Privileged Slattern?"

Slattern. Taniel recognized the name—a mid-ranking Privileged sorcerer in the Kez cabal. Taniel ignored the question and waited in silence, keeping his eyes on the swamp.

Nearly a full minute passed before a short, slight figure emerged from the cypress trees further up the hummock. She was a member of the Palo tribe that had been helping Taniel and his company of irregulars in the war against the Kez. Though she looked like a Palo, with bright red hair and skin covered in ashen freckles, she was an outsider, like him, and her strained relationship with her tribe meant she had become his constant companion here in Fatrasta.

Her small build always made Taniel think of her as young,

barely a teenager, but there was a clever defiance in her green eyes that always left him a little uneasy. Besides, he'd seen what she could do with the machete strapped to her thigh.

A bit of reed stuck out from between her teeth, and the front of her buckskins were soaked with blood.

"It's your lucky day, Jibble," Taniel said to the soldier.

"Sir?"

Taniel jerked his chin at the girl. "You got me instead of her. What took you so long, Pole?"

Ka-poel grinned at him in that way that he found unnerving, gesturing at the blood on her buckskins.

"The other guard?" he asked.

She drew a thumb across her throat, meeting Jibble's eyes as she did. The soldier swallowed hard, glancing from Taniel to Ka-poel as if he wasn't sure who to fear most. Ka-poel pointed at Jibble, cocking an eyebrow at Taniel.

"No," Taniel answered quietly, "we're not going to kill him. Not if he's smart."

Ka-poel gave a casual shrug, as if she didn't care one way or the other.

"Their camp?" Taniel asked.

Ka-poel pointed, then held up ten fingers. A hundred yards due east, on a big hummock that his own men used from time to time. It's back was to a deep channel, and its flanks were protected by almost impenetrable cypress groves. Not something Taniel wanted to fight through.

"All right." Taniel nudged Jibble gently in the small of his back with the barrel of his rifle. "Let's go nice and quiet. Pole, tell the others to get ready."

Ka-poel pursed her lips and gave a loud, shrill whistle, warbling it at the end like a glade sparrow. She waited three seconds, repeated the call, then waited another eight before doing it once more. The call was answered a moment later. Ka-poel gave Taniel a nod to proceed toward the Kez camp. She fell in beside him, her hands in lapels of her buckskin vest like she was a gentleman out for a stroll in a city park.

The camp was a collection of mud-caked tents and bedrolls tossed out on the hummock in an unorganized fashion. The stench of disease hung over it, and they passed a row of half a dozen men squatting over a shallow latrine, their heads between their knees, moaning pitifully. Taniel spotted three corpses tossed unceremoniously off to one side.

They were almost at the center of the camp before anyone noticed them. A soldier sitting on a root beside the largest of the tents looked up from his whittling, his eyes growing large.

"Enemy contact," he said in Kez, scrambling to his feet. "Enemy contact!" He produced a musket from behind his makeshift seat and leveled it at Taniel.

The camp fell out, men and women emerging from their tents or coming in from guard duty, muskets and swords at the ready. There was a general, panicked shouting as they searched for the enemy, looking every which way, expecting an army to come pouring out of the cypress.

An older gentleman emerged from the biggest tent. His shirt was undone at the collar and his face was pale, but his posture was impeccable as he pulled on his jacket, keeping a pistol in one hand at all times. A pair of pins on his jacket collar identified him as a major. He took stock of the situation at a glance, then eyed Ka-poel's bloody buckskins and gave Taniel a look up and down. He tossed the pistol away and took a long step from the closest soldier.

He'd heard the stories. He knew exactly what he was dealing with. "Order in the camp!" he bellowed.

Slowly, the chaos died down, and Taniel soon found himself staring down the barrels of at least fifty muskets, as well as the major's unwavering gaze.

"What's going on here?" the major demanded.

Private Jibble licked his lips. "Sorry, sir. He came upon me on guard, sir."

"Were you sleeping?"

"No, sir! He was as quiet as a… well, as a ghost, sir."

A murmur spread throughout the soldiers at the mention of the word "ghost." The Kez major considered this for a moment, then addressed Taniel in Adran. "Who are you and what are you doing in my camp?"

"My name," Taniel said, speaking loudly in Kez, "is Taniel Two-shot. I'm a captain with the Tristan Ghost Irregulars." There was a shuffle and creak as fingers tightened on triggers and footing was reassured. "In case you were wondering," Taniel continued. "I'm the one who killed your Privileged three days ago."

"We know who you bloody-well are, *powder mage*," the major said. "My name is Major Daxon je Buker and this is the 108th regiment of his majesty's Peacekeepers. You kill my guards and come into my camp with a loaded weapon? Give me one good reason why I shouldn't order my men to open fire."

"I'll give you two," Taniel said. "First off, *my* men have this hummock surrounded. Second, I could detonate all of your powder with a single thought, killing or wounding everyone here before they could pull their triggers."

"Then why haven't you already?" Buker asked.

"Because like you I'm a soldier. Not a butcher."

"You're a powder mage," Major Buker responded with more than a little disdain. "Don't pretend like you're one of the rank and file. Besides, if we were surrounded my guards would have notified me already."

"Like this one?" Taniel asked, poking Jibble in the small of the back.

Buker eyed Taniel and Ka-poel for a long moment, as if weighing his options. The muskets of his men had already begun to waver, but there was a steely stubborness in Buker's eyes that made Taniel a little bit nervous. To be honest, he'd be hard-pressed to detonate all of their powder simultaneously.

It took a lot of concentration to do so and a spark would very likely reach its bullet before he could warp the blast.

And powder mages weren't immune to bullets no matter the propellant.

Beside him, Ka-poel mimed shooting Buker with a pistol. "You're not helping," he told her quietly.

Buker shot her a look of disgust. Kez nobles rarely thought much of the local savages. Taniel's time among the Palo had taught him that the feeling was mutual. He didn't have to wonder how long Buker would last if left along in the swamp with Ka-poel.

"Surely you know why we're here?" Buker asked, clasping his hands behind his back and thrusting out his chest.

"To take my head to the Kez governor, I'd assume," Taniel said. It wasn't the first company the Kez had sent into Tristan Basin to find him and his irregulars, and it wouldn't be the last.

"We're here to hunt you, and you'd still accept our surrender?"

"Certainly. War is war. No hard feelings, and all that."

Taniel shifted his aim slightly so that the bullet would go under Jibble's arm and strike Buker in the chest if he was forced to pull the trigger. If this all went to shit, he would take the major down with him.

Buker didn't seem to notice. He looked around the camp, his eyes lingering on the men who didn't have the energy to pull themselves off the latrine even in the case of an alarm. "If we surrender," Buker said, "I expect my men and I to be properly cared for as prisoners of war, and ransomed as soon as possible."

"Agreed," Taniel said.

Buker's chin sagged. "In that case, I formally surrender. Men, lower your arms!"

The sighs of relief amongst the soldiers were audible as muskets and swords were dropped.

"Major Bertreau," Taniel called into the swamp. "You may relieve the Kez of their arms!"

Dozens of men in buckskins, bayonets fixed on their rifles, emerged from the trees and began to round up the Kez, gathering their weapons and supplies for inventory. They were accompanied by an equal number of their Palo allies. Taniel watched them work their way through the camp, noting the way the Palo studiously avoided Ka-poel, before he allowed himself to let out a quiet sigh and lower his rifle.

Sergeant Mapel, a squat, dusty-skinned bulldog of a man with a neck like a tree trunk, was the first to approach Taniel. He took Buker's sword and pistol, grinning broadly. "Good work, captain," he said.

"Thanks. Go easy on them. I don't see any of *their* Palo guides. If I had to guess, they were abandoned right about the time they all started coming down with dysentery. Would have been a piss-poor fight if it had come down to it." Taniel glanced at Ka-poel and shouldered his weapon. She shook her head. She didn't see any enemy Palo either.

Mapel shrugged. "Still think you should have just picked 'em off, one by one."

Taniel had no love for the Kez, but his own ire tended to be directed at the Privileged and nobility. He didn't need to kill *every* common soldier he came across. Unlike Mapel.

"What should we do with them?" Mapel asked, nodding at the Kez prisoners.

Taniel pursed his lips. "Give them a dozen Palo guards and send them down to Gladeside. Sooner they're out of our hair, the better."

"Yes, sir."

"Where's the major?" Taniel looked around, realizing he had yet to spot Bertreau.

"Called back to camp"

"For what?"

"We've word from the outside. Seems the Kez are on the

move in our neck of the woods—or swamp, as it may be—and they're planning for something big. Supposedly there's a whole brigade on the Basin Highway."

Taniel was already heading toward a canoe before Mapel had finished his sentence.

The Kez had yet to mobilize any large forces this far inland. If they were, it couldn't mean anything good for the Tristan Ghost Irregulars. "Pole!" he shouted over his shoulder. "Come on!"

The Ghost Irregulars were camped on a hummock about a mile southeast of the Kez. It wasn't as good of a position as the Kez had chosen, but it was far better organized. There were no fire or latrine pits to mark their passing, and the men slept in hammocks with mosquito netting, few of them further than a dozen paces from their canoes.

The camp was quiet when Taniel and Ka-poel pulled their canoe onto the hummock. One of the few remaining guards—a lad of no more than fifteen named Heln—tipped his tricorn hat and took Taniel's kit and rifle. "How'd the raid go, captain?" Taniel nodded in return. Heln had been with them since the beginning. He couldn't shoot worth a damn, but he had sharp eyes and ears. Watching him try to flirt with Ka-poel was one of Taniel's favorite pastimes.

"Well enough," Taniel said. "Only casualty was one of the Kez guards." He looked across at an unfamiliar canoe lying in the mud. "Whose is that?"

Heln ducked his head toward the only tent on the hummock, which belonged to Major Bertreau. Just as he opened his mouth, a figure stepped out of the tent, putting on a fur cap, and strode toward Taniel.

He was an older man, with a grizzled beard grown to mid-chest. He wore the same frontiersmen fashion as Taniel, but the fringe on his buckskins was mostly worn away and the knees and elbows had long since been patched and repatched. He had the scarred, weather-beaten complexion of one who'd been out in the bush for a long, long time. Maybe an explorer, or a trapper, but either way it explained how he'd managed to find the Ghost Irregulars.

Taniel extended a hand as the stranger approached. "Good afternoon," he said, hoping to get a quick word about what was happening back in civilization.

The stranger glanced at Taniel, then Ka-poel, his gaze remaining on her for long enough that Taniel almost called him out for it. Then he moved on, ignoring Taniel's hand as he tossed his kit into the bottom of his canoe and pulled it out into the water. In moments he was gone, paddling through the cypress.

Taniel watched him go, scowling, then exchanged a look with Ka-poel. She shrugged.

The flap to Bertreau's tent was thrown back again, and the major appeared. She was a slender woman in her mid-thirties with tired gray eyes. She wore the yellow uniform of the Fatrastan militia instead of the buckskins the Palo supplied, and had scarring all around the base of her neck—a story Taniel still hoped to get out of her some day.

"Heln!" she bellowed, fanning her face with her tricorn. "So bloody hot out here. Heln, send someone to fetch Two-shot, I..." she paused. "Oh. You're here already. Good. Is that asshole gone?"

Taniel glanced the way the stranger had left. "Took off," he said.

"Double-good." Bertreau shook her head. "I don't know where they dig these people up. Trappers make great scouts, but some of them spend years without talking to another person and it addles their wits."

"And their manners," Taniel said.

"Don't get me started. Did you take the Kez camp?"

"We did. The boys are cleaning it up as we speak. We're

sending the prisoners to Gladeside with a Palo guard."

"Good, good," Bertreau said dismissively. "Glad it went quick."

Taniel scowled. They'd been tracking the Kez for two weeks now, and all she had to say was 'good'? He jerked his head toward where the messenger had disappeared into the cypress. "What news did we get?"

"News?" Bertreau asked. "Nothing. Asshole didn't even bring us the post. We did get orders, however."

It was Taniel's turn to make a sour face. The bit about the post stung. Unlike the others, he wasn't just a few hundred miles from where he'd grown up. He was an ocean away from home. It had been nearly a year, and he had no way of knowing if news had reached his fiancée or father that he'd joined the war.

"Orders?" he asked. "I was beginning to think there wasn't anybody in charge of this war."

Bertreau rolled her eyes at him and removed a worn envelope from her jacket pocket. The paper was brown and faded, curled on the edges from the humidity, and the broken seal was in the shape of a rose on white wax. "We've been out here a long time, but not that long. Governor Lindet is still in power. She's calling herself Lady Chancellor now— not sure if I like the sound of that, but not much I can do about it."

She coughed, hacked, then hawked a wad of phlegm onto the ground before examining the letter in her hand and continuing. "The Kez are making a move on Planth."

Planth wasn't a large city—maybe ten thousand people or so—but it was the biggest in the Basin and a fairly major trading post on the Tristan River. If you wanted to get to the northwest wilds where all the best hunting and trapping were, you had to go through Planth. It was easily accessible by road and rivers for the average settler or frontiersmen— less so to a fully-equipped army.

Even still, Taniel was less surprised by the news than he was by the timing. "They've left Planth alone so far. Why are they moving on it?"

"No idea," Bertreau said. "Not sure about you, but in my experience orders rarely come with an explanation as to the motives of one's enemies."

Taniel felt his cheeks color. He liked Bertreau well enough, and he knew she liked him, but she also enjoyed reminding him how little real combat experience he had outside of hunting Kez through the Basin these last twelve months.

"When?" he asked.

"There's an army coming up the Basin Highway at this very moment," Bertreau said, consulting the letter. "They're a week away from the city. Scouts say a full brigade. Maybe more."

Five thousand infantry, probably accompanied by horse, three or four Privileged sorcerers, and auxiliaries. Last Taniel heard, Planth had a garrison of five hundred irregulars holed up in the old trader fort at the bend of the river. The fort was meant to fend off raids from hostile Palo, not a modern army with artillery and sorcery. It would be wiped out in a single afternoon.

He let out a low whistle. "Well," he said, "there goes our source of provisions. I hope they're evacuating Planth because there won't be anything left by the end of next week. What are our orders? Pull deeper into the Basin?"

Bertreau snorted. "I wish," she said, slapping the letter against her palm. "These orders call every able-bodied Fatrastan regiment in the region to the defense of Planth."

Taniel felt his mouth hanging open. When the war began, the Fatrastan army would be hard-pressed to put together a whole brigade of real soldiers all together, and maybe three or four times that many in irregulars. Unless there were fifty companies just like his hiding out in the Basin, Planth didn't stand a chance.

It was a damned foolish order.

He felt the elation of the afternoon's victory disappear, leaving him with a nervous pit in his stomach. Based on the look on Bertreau's face, she was thinking the same thing.

"What," Bertreau said quietly, "are we supposed to do against an entire brigade of Kez soldiers?"

Taniel took the orders from Bertreau and looked them over. They were signed by Lady Chancellor Lindet herself, stressing the importance of not allowing the Kez army to reach Planth. "Proceed up the Basin Highway," Taniel read aloud, "directly to Planth to aid in the city's defense. Do not delay."

Ka-poel tapped Taniel on the shoulder.

"What is it?" he asked.

She pointed to herself, then Taniel and Bertreau, and then held her fist above her head, face twisted, to mime a hangman's noose.

"Yes," Taniel agreed, "it sounds like it's going to get us killed."

Ka-poel cocked a half-smile at him and shook her head like he didn't understand. She ran to Taniel's hammock and came back a moment later with his sketchbook, flipping through the pages until she found the map he'd made of the Tristan Basin. She pointed at Planth, then at their current location, and finally at the Basin Highway.

She drew a line with her finger from their approximate position across to the road. The tapped the road twice, then bent and wrote the Palo word for "Kez" in the dirt.

"What's she all on about?" Bertreau asked, angling her head to read the map. No one but Taniel ever seemed to catch on to Ka-poel's silent speech, and even he had a hard time with it.

Taniel did some math in his head, based on where the orders claimed the Kez were currently located, along with the fact that the orders were already four days old. "She's telling us where we are in relation to this army."

"So?" Bertreau asked.

Taniel thought he knew what Ka-poel was getting at. She wasn't afraid of getting killed—she was out for blood. "She's saying we can avoid getting trapped inside Planth."

"I'm not running away from an order," Bertreau said.

"No, we wouldn't run away. Look, we're skirmishers. We'll do no one any good behind the walls of the fort or holding the line outside the city. But we're not all that far from the Kez army. Instead of going straight to Planth we head over and harass the Kez. It'll slow them down and give Planth more time to prepare."

Bertreau pursed her lips. "Not exactly following orders."

"We'll be following the spirit of them. And doing what we do best."

A slow smile spread on Bertreau's face. "We'll strike from the shadows like ghosts."

Taniel sat in the stern of his canoe, legs crossed, drawing in his sketchbook with a bit of charcoal he kept in his pocket for quiet moments. He drew Ka-poel, her head in profile, back silhouetted by rays of the early morning sun streaming through the mist. He wished he had colored charcoal so he could capture her fiery hair or the way her skin seemed to redden when she faced the sun.

It was early in the morning, just a day and a half after they'd received their orders, and the Ghost Irregulars waited for their scouts to report in.

Every so often Taniel would flip the page and add a few details to his drawing of Bertreau, stealing furtive glances toward her canoe whenever she wasn't looking. It wasn't nearly as good as those he did of Ka-poel; the nose was all wrong and the angle of her face was off. But he always had to work quickly on it. Ka-poel liked having her portrait done.

Bertreau… not so much.

A figure emerged from the morning mist and approached Bertreau's canoe—it was Milgi, one of the Palo scouts. He and Bertreau conferred for a moment before she gestured to Taniel.

Taniel put away his sketchbook and paddled up beside Bertreau, planting the paddle firmly in the muck. He removed a snuff box from his jacket and tapped a line of black powder on the back of his hand, snorting it with one nostril. The whole world came alive as sorcery coursed through him, magnifying the sights and sounds of the swamp, making his limbs eager for action. He took a few deep breaths to calm the powder trance, reveling in the clarity of mind it brought him.

"We're closer to the Kez than we thought," Bertreau said.

"How far?" Taniel asked.

Milgi glared at Ka-poel for a few moments before answering. "Two miles," he said in broken Adran. He went back to glaring. Most of the Palo were rude to Ka-poel, if not outright hostile. She was a foreigner, a Dynize from the west, and though she had been raised by the Palo only her abilities as a sorcerer kept her from being banished.

Taniel wasn't even sure what those abilities were, beyond that it helped her track his enemies. He'd given up trying to understand her relationship with her adopted tribe or her sorcery. He simply found that her presence had become reassuring.

"And how long does their baggage train stretch?" he asked.

Milgi paused to think, his lips moving as he translated the words in his head. "About four miles."

"They're moving slowly," Taniel said to Bertreau. "Vulnerable and stretched out. We can pick at them with hardly a risk."

Bertreau hummed thoughtfully, her eyes wandering the swamp. She shook her head. "I don't like it. Five thousand or more men, plus Privileged. I don't know if I want to risk the Ghost Irregulars for that."

"I can take care of the Privileged," Taniel said with more confidence than he felt. Privileged fell to a well-placed bullet just like anyone else and as a powder mage, he could hit them from more than a mile away. The trick was not to miss the first shot and give the Privileged time to respond with elemental sorcery. "We're going to have to face the Kez sometime," Taniel continued. "It might as well be here, in our territory, and not in formation outside of Planth. Hardly any of our boys have ever seen a proper infantry line, let alone drilled for one. We fight now and we have a better chance of walking away."

"We can't kill them all before they reach Planth. There's five thousand of them."

"Yeah," Taniel countered. "But we can soften them up for the defenders."

Bertreau cleared her throat, looking back at the long line of canoes stretching back into the swamp behind them, irregulars and their Palo allies crouched in each one, waiting for orders.

"Stash the canoes," Bertreau finally said. "And you, Two-shot, take your savage and scout us out some good targets. Looks like we'll be nipping at heels for the next few days."

T aniel waited in the darkness, water lapping at his thighs, the unsteady sound of his own breathing forming a familiar rhythm. He had a new hole in his moccasin—he could tell because the toes of his right foot were clammy and cold, water sloshing between them every time he shifted on his haunches. That was going to get annoying really damn quick.

The swamp was quiet—at least, as quiet as a swamp would normally get. Bullfrogs croaked in the distance behind him while he listened to the quiet chatting of a pair of Kez soldiers discussing their lovers back in the homeland. To anyone else, the words were just a low buzz at almost thirty yards, but Taniel's trance-enhanced ears could hear every lurid detail and he felt his cheeks warm slightly.

Ka-poel shifted beside him, touching him gently to keep her balance. Taniel exchanged a glance with her but she was, as usual, placid and unreadable. He wondered if she ever felt any real fear, or if all of this was some kind of a game to her. He wondered if he'd ever actually know.

To his right Taniel could make out the hunched forms of over a dozen of the Ghost Irregulars waiting for his signal.

Taniel wished he'd brought his canteen—his throat was as dry as the pit—but by necessity he didn't have anything on him but his belt knife and a powder horn. He held the knife in one hand, gripping it tightly, feeling naked without his rifle.

He remembered his father telling stories to him as a boy about sneaking into Gurlish fortresses to spike their cannons in order to break a siege. Taniel had played with his friends, pretending to be an Adran soldier doing the same, getting away by the skin of his teeth or dying in a blaze of glory.

It felt strange to remember such fantasies when he was here, now, preparing to do essentially the same thing.

His mind was brought back to the present by the movement of a torch bobbing through the swamp toward his hiding place. He lowered himself an extra couple of inches, watching the shadowy outline of his companions do the same. Only Ka-poel didn't flinch, remaining as still as a stone.

The torch continued along, not wavering in its path parallel to the Basin Highway where the Kez had made their camp, and Taniel looked pointedly away from the source of the flame, focusing instead on the face beneath it. It belonged to an older soldier, his musket over his shoulder, peering into the night with a look of consternation. His gaze swept across

Taniel and the Ghost Irregulars without stopping before he continued on.

Never, Taniel thought to himself, *hold the torch in front of you. It ruins your vision.*

The night wore on, Kez fires growing dim as the moon rose high into the sky, casting patches of light across the waters of the swamp. It wasn't long before the distant sounds of conversation and soldiers going about their nightly routines disappeared. The new silence was punctuated from time to time by Kez camp guards stomping through the underbrush.

After one of the patrols had passed, Taniel finally rose to his feet, shaking out his limbs one at a time to get the blood moving and loosen aching joints. He snorted a pinch of powder, feeling the sorcery sharpen his night vision.

"It's time," he said softly.

The words were passed down the line, and the rest of the Ghost Irregulars rose up, clutching their knives, limbering up for their task. Taniel felt a thrill go through him. They'd stalked, captured, and killed hundreds of Kez but they had never faced a true force of soldiers like this before.

Taniel motioned with his knife hand and crept through the water, watching as the Ghost Irregulars split off into groups of three or four. He almost called them back, feeling a pang of last-minute trepidation, but he bit his tongue.

This is what they did best.

He and Ka-poel emerged from the swamp water onto the firm-packed soil of the highway and waited until the count of sixty before heading forward.

The highway itself was little more than a stretch of naturally hard soil, shored up over the centuries by locals, that stretched the length of the Tristan Basin. In some places the hard-pack was a mile across, in others scarcely a few feet, but it provided a reliable passage for traders and settlers through the Basin.

Taniel and his men had scouted well, finding a place where

the highway was only about half a dozen yards across. A disturbance here would effectively divide the long, snaking camp in two.

But Taniel had more in mind than just a disturbance.

"Remember," he whispered to Ka-poel, handing her flint and tinder, "don't light their powder."

It was only a few paces to the nearest wagons, yet in the tense final moments before an attack, the distance seemed like miles. He crept along, listening to the snores of the teamsters sleeping nearby, and reached out with his senses. The wagon was packed with several barrels of black powder—a prime target for any saboteur, let alone a powder mage. But that wasn't what he needed right now. He moved on to the next wagon, then the next, until he found a feed wagon with bales of hay and alfalfa for the horses.

Perfect.

Taniel emptied a few lines of black powder from his horn beside one of the bales. He lit the powder with a thought and watched it fizz, hissing to life. He gently blew the embers into the hay. Within seconds a great tower of smoke rose from the cart. He waited a few moments until he heard shouting from somewhere down the baggage train where the rest of the Ghost Irregulars were setting their own fires, and then shouted in Kez,

"Fire, fire!"

Teamsters sprang from their wagons, stumbling out of their bedrolls, panicked cries going up among them. Taniel, undetected, ran to the edge of the swamp. He paused for a moment, checking to be sure Ka-poel had escaped, only to spot a pair of skinny legs sticking out from beneath a nearby wagon. Taniel swore to himself and sprinted back toward her. "Let's go, Pole," he growled, grabbing her by the ankles.

Ka-poel's head appeared, and she bared her teeth at him, slapping away his hands, and then ducked back beneath the wagon. Taniel could hear the sound of her flint striking and realized she'd yet to get her own fire going.

"No time for that now!" Taniel said, grabbing her by one foot.

She kicked him away, there was the sound of the flint several more times, and then she suddenly scrambled out from beneath the wagon, followed closely by a thin trial of smoke. Taniel helped her to her feet.

"You there!" a voice shouted, and Taniel turned in time to see a teamster grabbing at Ka-poel's shoulder. Taniel threw a wild punch across the man's jaw and Ka-poel kicked him between the legs. They left him an angry, swearing mess as they sprinted for the cover of the swamp.

The cypresses were lit by an orange glow as the blaze consumed the camp. Taniel could hear the frenzied dash of the other Ghost Irregulars making their escape, and the shouts of Kez teamsters and soldiers as they sought to douse the flames that enveloped at least ten of their wagons.

After about two hundred yards, Taniel stopped running and began to frantically search the bases of the cypress, looking for a knife mark on the roots of one of the bigger trees. A panic struck him as he failed to find the mark, and he feared that he'd gotten turned around in the darkness. Sweat broke out on his brow. All of this waiting and work was for nothing if he couldn't find the mark. He swore to himself quietly. "Pole. Pole! Where's the damn tree?"

There was no answer—not that he expected one—but when he looked around, Ka-poel was no longer at his heels.

"Captain," a low voice said, "is everything okay?"

Taniel found Sergeant Mapel nearby, gasping from his run, leaning against a cypress root.

"It's fine," Taniel spat. "I'm just looking for that damned tree."

Mapel sucked on his teeth, glancing around at the myriad of cypress that surrounded them. He didn't have the sorcery that allowed him to see in the dark, not like Taniel, and would be no help at all. "You know the drill, captain," Mapel said. "If you can't find it, we get out of here. No sense taking needless risks."

"Go on," Taniel said. "I'll be close behind."

"I'll wait for you."

"No," Taniel said. "Get to the rendezvous. That's an order. Make sure all our boys made it out."

Mapel nodded reluctantly and headed deeper into the swamp. Taniel swore to himself, watching the sergeant go. Mapel was right, of course. No needless risks.

A sharp whistle caught Taniel's attention. He looked up and, after a moment of searching, found Ka-poel sitting in the high branches of one of the cypress trees not a stone's throw away. Taniel felt a wave of relief wash over him. He sprinted over and climbed the tree, checking the knife mark on the way up. This was it, all right.

A cautious climber could make it to the top of one of the big cypress in just a few minutes. Taniel threw that caution to the wind, scrambling up the thick, winding branches until he was at the very top. He found Ka-poel waiting for him, holding out the kit and rifle he'd stashed here earlier.

Ka-poel mimed that the rifle was already loaded.

"Two bullets?" Taniel asked.

She nodded.

Taniel swung around, wrapping his legs around a branch and giving himself a comfortable seat from which to aim. He brought the stock to his shoulder and sighted down the length of the rifle.

The height of the old cypress allowed him a commanding vision of all the tree-tops for miles around but, more importantly, it allowed him a clear view of the Basin Highway and the Kez army camped along it. He could see the fires raging through the baggage train, the dry wood of the old wagons catching as easily as cotton, and felt a momentary pang of pity for the poor sods rushing to put out the flames.

If he knew the Kez command structure, at least one teamster would hang for this.

He pushed away the thought and focused on the task at hand, reaching out with his senses for the wagon of black powder that he'd first approached. He found it easily and noted that the teamsters had already moved it well away from the flames.

In his mind, he designated the powder barrels as target one.

"Powder," he said, holding out one hand. He felt Kapoel put a fresh powder charge in his palm, and tore the end off without looking, emptying the contents straight into his mouth. The taste was bitter and sulfuric, the granules crunching between his teeth, but the effect of so much powder was instantaneous.

It felt as if time had slowed to a crawl. Every one of his senses brought the details of the world into sharp focus, allowing him to hear and see everything going on down in the Kez camp as if he was standing down there among them. He felt as if his heart would explode from the rush of adrenaline and his mind would be overwhelmed by all the sensory information, but the nature of his sorcery allowed him to bring it all under control.

He forced himself to focus, moving his aim up and down the length of the camp, reaching out with his senses until he found the Privileged sorcerer walking through the camp.

Even now, after killing several Privileged, he still felt a chill run down his spine when he put one in his sights. It was as if they could see him aiming at them from the distance and were about to raise their hands, twitching gloved fingers to call sorcery into this world and snuff him out as easily as a candle.

Privileged were, blow for blow, far more powerful than powder mages. But of the advantages that a powder mage had over a Privileged one of the most important was that

Taniel could sense a Privileged while a Privileged could *not* sense him.

"Target two," he whispered to himself.

The seconds ticked by as the Privileged got closer to the fires. A dozen bodyguards clustered around him, eyes on the surrounding swamp, their caution well-warranted. They spread out a bit as their master reached the baggage train and raised his gloved hands, summoning water and wind to do his bidding and put out the fires.

Taniel pulled the trigger.

In his mind's eye, Taniel burned black powder to control the trajectories of the two bullets leaving the muzzle of his rifle. He adjusted the flight of the first bullet minutely, nudging it slightly up and to the left as it cut through the air and slammed into the center of the Privileged's chest.

At the same time, he corrected the wobbling flight of the second bullet and sent it straight into the wagon of powder barrels.

The resulting explosion would have knocked him out of his perch had Ka-poel not steadied him by the back of his collar. He took a deep breath, his ears ringing from the sound, and watched the resulting chaos for several moments before handing Ka-poel his rifle and shimmying down the tree.

It would be several hours before anyone figured out that the Privileged had died from a bullet to the sternum and not from the explosion. The longer the Kez went without realizing there was a powder mage nearby, the better.

Two days after he killed the Privileged, Taniel watched from the vantage of a cypress tree as a pair of his companions fled into the woods, followed by at least thirty Kez soldiers. It was late in the evening, and he and the Ghost Irregulars had managed three more strikes, varying their tactics each time.

This strike had been different. Only a couple of Ghost Irregulars went in, getting close enough to assassinate a pair of guards. It was impetuous and sloppy and undertaken in the daylight, as if they were getting overconfident.

Just as it was meant to look.

Taniel sighted down his rifle, waiting for the pursuing Kez soldiers to get closer. But they came to a slow stop, firing their muskets and shouting a few choice words after the Ghost Irregulars, before turning back and retreating to their camp. He watched them go, disappointed, before climbing down from his hiding spot and heading to find Major Bertreau.

The major was with the rest of the Ghost Irregulars, spaced out around a hollow a few hundred yards distant, waiting in what would have been a perfect ambush for the Kez pursuers.

"They didn't take the bait," Taniel told her.

Bertreau swore. "We might have been too obvious."

"They didn't take the bait last night, either."

Bertreau scowled into the trees, as if trying to will the Kez to fall into her trap. "They're catching on to us."

"They must have someone smart in charge for once," Taniel replied. The Kez had a habit of putting their idiot, inbred nobility in command of their colonial armies. But that didn't mean they should be underestimated, or that quality officers didn't wind up with a command from time to time.

"Had to happen sooner or later," Bertreau said. "Mapel! Have everyone fall back." She jerked her head to one side, pulling Taniel away from the rest of the soldiers as they prepared to leave. "I've been thinking," she said quietly, "about our orders."

"What about them?" Taniel asked.

"Have you considered what they actually meant?"

"Sure. They wanted us to return to Planth. But we decided to come here and delay the Kez instead."

"Not that," Bertreau said. "What they *meant*! Think about

it. The Kez sending a whole brigade into the Tristan Basin? Planth calling for every available regiment? There's something important in Planth."

Taniel stared at her. Two days straight of running a powder trance left his brain a little wired, and he was having trouble following Bertreau's logic.

"Those orders were only four days old when we got them," Bertreau said, "and they were signed by Lindet herself. Our damned chancellor is *hiding in Planth*."

Taniel didn't know a lot about the politics behind the Fatrastan Revolution but what he knew was that one of the local governors, Lindet, spearheaded the movement and was now in charge of the new government. She was outnumbered and outgunned by the Kez colonial armies and so she and her staff kept moving, always hiding.

And this time, apparently, the Kez had found her.

He cursed himself quietly for not seeing it earlier. Planth was far more important than he'd initially suspected. Lindet and her staff were the spine of the revolution. If this brigade reached Planth, the government would be captured and the war—Fatrastan independence and everything Taniel and his companions had fought for—would be over.

The thought troubled him the whole way back to camp. All of their efforts had barely slowed the Kez brigade, buying Planth perhaps an extra day to prepare. But the Kez were bent on reaching Planth, and they were not taking any bait that might distract them. A few hundred extra casualties meant nothing to them.

The Ghost Irregulars reached camp, breaking out the rations for a late dinner while men shook the spiders out of their hammocks. Taniel wished, not for the first time, that they were far enough from the enemy to make camp fires.

He sat down on a log next to Ka-poel and chewed his sausages and stale biscuits without relish, considering the options available to them. They could continue their tactics all the way to Planth—another three days' march—and then harry them as they took the city. But beyond that, the Ghost Irregulars were helpless. They weren't much use in a pitched battle, which this whole thing would no-doubt come down to.

So what else could they do to delay the Kez? Send a few squads to go on ahead, blocking the path with fallen trees? But there were still more Privileged with the Kez brigade— now hiding themselves from Taniel—and they could sweep aside any obstacle with a gesture.

It made Taniel feel helpless.

His increasingly negative thoughts were cut off by a distant call from one of the camp guards.

"Rider coming in!"

Taniel exchanged a glance with Ka-poel and snatched up his rifle before he went looking for Bertreau. He found the major having her own dinner beside her tent. "Did someone just say a rider was coming in?" she asked.

"I was just about to ask you the same thing," Taniel replied. Together, they walked to the edge of the camp, gathering a small crowd as they waited to see what type of bloody fool would ride a horse through this swamp dragon-infested mire. More than a few of the Ghost Irregulars had armed themselves, and even Ka-poel had a hand on her machete. Taniel was the first to spot a flash of metal moving through the trees.

"See him?" Bertreau asked.

"I… I think so? But I might be going mad."

A few moments passed before Bertreau let out a long breath. "No. No, I definitely see it too."

A horse waded through the knee-deep water. It was the biggest horse Taniel had ever seen, easily twenty hands high with the powerful build of a true war animal. Interlocking plate armor covered its head, neck, and hindquarters, while a skirt of mail gently skimmed the water.

A horse that size would make any man seem small, but the rider on its back looked shockingly proportional. He was similarly armored, encased in leather, plate, and mail that must weigh eight stone, and had both hands on the reins, a long, wooden lance under one arm with a cavalry sword sheathed on his left side and a carbine holstered on his right.

No one, not even heavy cuirassiers, wore armor like that any more. The whole thing was like a vision out a fairy tale, with a warrior two and a half centuries out of date.

A familiar tingle went down Taniel's spine as the horse emerged from the water to stand, barely looking affected by all that weight, staring Taniel down like he was a bug to be stomped. Sorcery radiated off the creature, and it took him several moments to realize it wasn't coming from the horse or the rider, but rather the armor that they wore.

Pit-damned enchanted armor. No one wore armor that looked like that any more, and no one enchanted much of anything, either.

The rider shifted, lifting a sack out of his saddlebags, tossing it on the ground at their feet. The sack was soaked through with blood, and a head rolled out of it to come to a rest at Bertreau's toe. The face was fixed in a gruesome expression, the neck cut cleanly. By the size of the sack, there were two more heads inside.

"Kresimir," Bertreau swore. Taniel couldn't help but echo the oath silently.

"Kez are tracking you," the rider said in a throaty growl, voice echoing from his helmet. He flipped up the visor, gazing down at Taniel and Bertreau with an expression only slightly less intimidating than his horse. "I'm looking for Major Bertreau."

Bertreau, for the year that Taniel had known her, was fairly unflappable. She was more liable to show anger than fear, and not a lot impressed her. Her eyes still fixed on the severed head, she gave a low whistle before finally looking up at the rider.

"Reporting," Bertreau said, snapping a salute. She elbowed Taniel in the ribs and reluctantly he threw up his own salute, still trying to get his mind around what he saw before him. A man with severed heads in a sack, riding a fully-armored warhorse into a damned swamp like it was a ride in the countryside, wearing enchanted armor! The armor, he decided, was the hardest part to get over.

The big man surveying the camp, nodding slowly to himself. His face was handsome in an open, honest sort of way, worn rough by the elements and criss-crossed with scars. Dirty-blond hair was matted to his forehead with sweat. Taniel guessed he was in his mid-thirties. "I'm Colonel Ben Styke. You assholes are a pain to find."

"That's kind of the point, sir," Taniel said. Inwardly, he repeated Bertreau's whistle. He should have recognized that armor from the stories. Mad Ben Styke and his Mad Lancers were a damned legend. Rumors said they were a company of volunteer cavalrymen who'd looted a Kez governor's collection of ancient cavalry armor and taken to wearing the stuff. Taniel never really believed it. And he certainly hadn't guessed that the armor was enchanted. Bloody pit.

"Pole, what are you... " Taniel wasn't able to catch her in time as Ka-poel slipped past him and approached the horse.

"Careful, girl," Styke said. "He'll bite your whole hand off."

Ka-poel seemed less than worried. She patted the beast's armored nose, rubbing its exposed neck beneath the armor. The horse shook its head, then leaned into her for a nuzzle that almost planted her on her ass.

"I'll be damned," Styke said. "He doesn't like many people, girl. Take that as an honor." He leaned over Ka-poel, sniffing, then turned toward Taniel. "You smell of powder and sorcery. You must be Taniel Two-shot."

"That's me," Taniel said, lifting his chin. He'd known

plenty of big men like this in the Adran Army—grenadiers, usually—and they rarely respected anything but strength. Someone this size would ride all over you unless you took a stand.

"Good," Styke said, his face suddenly splitting in a grin. "Pleasure to meet you. Heard you've been popping Privileged left and right, and for that I owe you a drink."

Taniel opened his mouth with a retort that died on his tongue. "I, uh... thank you, sir."

"Thank me when you've got a drink in hand," Styke said. "Could be a while. Lindet appreciates what you've been doing down here to slow the Kez, but you," he nodded to Bertreau and the rest of the camp, "are needed in Planth immediately."

"She knows we're here?" Taniel asked.

"Lindet knows just about everything. She's got spies crawling out her ass. We best get moving soon, though.

Bertreau looked around, and Taniel could tell she was more than a little star-struck. This was Ben Styke, after all. In the flesh. Taniel, despite his sorcery, was feeling more than a little intimidated himself. Not that he'd ever admit it.

"It's getting late," Bertreau said. "It'll be dark within the hour."

"Just enough time to pack the camp and get moving," Styke replied. He leaned forward, banging his mailed fist against the armor on his mount's neck. "We've got twenty-five miles to make before noon tomorrow. Best get started."

Taniel exchanged another look with Bertreau. After all their work, they still had to head to Planth. And no getting around a direct order this time. He headed toward his hammock. "Camp!" he called. "Get ready to move!"

The Ghost Irregulars skirted the Kez army in the darkness, taking the river north toward Planth. They lost Styke during the night, but by the time they finally hid their canoes and made their way over to the Basin Highway, he was already waiting for them atop his enormous warhorse, ready to accompany them the last couple of miles.

For someone who'd been out in the swamps for almost a full year, the sight of Planth was like a light at the end of a long, wet, snake-infested tunnel. The Ghost Irregulars had ranged all over the Basin, passing through towns and forts to re-provision, send post, and get their orders, but Planth was almost big enough to be a proper city.

Built atop of a stony ridge jutting from the swamps, it had begun as a trading fort on a bend in the Tristan River and had grown into a hamlet, then a town, and now boasted almost ten thousand settlers of a dozen different nationalities, including a fair number of Palo. Land for miles around had been cleared and drained for farming. While the fort still dominated the stony ridge, the city itself sprawled along the side of the river, unprotected by walls or palisades.

Taniel was surprised to see an enormous camp on the outskirts of the city. There were hundreds of tents, impromptu stables, hastily-built outhouses, and all the trappings of an army at rest that would have made him think of home had it not been so hodge-podge. No dozen tents were the same color and so many different flags were raised above the camp he lost count.

He could tell at a glance this was not an army. This was a hastily-gathered militia pulled from the nearest towns and outposts. It would fall beneath the Kez brigade in a few hours—sooner, if the Kez unleashed their remaining Privileged.

Bertreau sent Taniel on with Styke, opting to go looking for a tavern with the parting words, "You're the Privileged-killing hero. You deal with the politicians."

The city was crowded, shoulder-to-shoulder. Men wearing the dark yellow coats of the Fatrastan Continental Army rubbed shoulders with buckskin-clad frontiersmen, plain-clothed settlers, and fancily-dressed businessmen. Practically everyone had a musket or rifle on their shoulder and a fight in their eyes, and Taniel allowed himself to be led through it all by Styke. Ka-poel tagged along at his heels, barely keeping up.

"Are we in that much of a hurry?" Taniel asked. "This place is chaos. I'd like to ask around for news from home."

"Chancellor first," Styke replied. "I don't worry about keeping her waiting but you probably should." He paused at a crossroad and pointed forward. "I've got to go stable my horse. Go straight on till you find the big church and tell them you're to see Lindet immediately."

Abandoned, Taniel and Ka-poel shoved and cursed through the press. While she was utterly undeterred by Styke or his enormous warhorse, Ka-poel seemed a little more intimidated by the sheer number of people. She was shoved and knocked around, and almost drew her machete on a passing frontiersmen, before Taniel finally planted her firmly behind him and told her to hang on to his belt.

Even with him leading, they got turned around twice before eventually made their way to the very center of the city where the square was dominated by big yellow tents, each of them waving the flag of the Continental Army. There seemed to be lines everywhere—a tangle of humanity streaming in and out of pubs, whorehouses, hotels, and privies.

There was a church on the northern side of the square, and even it had a line—a mix of soldiers, militiamen, and townsfolk, all waving orders or contracts, arguing amongst themselves. They were kept organized by a varied group of well-dressed city men in black vests and bowler caps. The line wrapped around the church twice, and Taniel stared glumly at the end before heading straight up to the big door.

"Taniel Two-shot to see Lindet," he said.

The big city man at the door looked like a whorehouse

bouncer. His eyes were even glued to the notebook in one hand, and he said without looking up, "You'll wait like the rest of the riff-raff. Back of the line."

Taniel glanced over his shoulder. He was *not* waiting for several hours to attend an urgent summons. "I'm with the Tristan Ghost Irregulars," he said. "We've been summoned by the Lady Chancellor."

"So has everyone else."

"Look, I was told…"

"I don't care what you've been told," the man said, finally looking up. "If I have to tell you to the back of the line once more I will knock in all those pretty white teeth of yours."

Taniel felt a spike of anger in his belly and stepped forward. "You want to try that?" he asked quietly.

"Boy, I will… " the man said, grabbing Taniel's lapels.

A voice cut him off. "Devan, are you talking back to my friends?"

Ben Styke appeared out of the crowd. He'd removed his armor, and now wore a yellow cavalry jacket, the stars of a colonel pinned proudly to one lapel, three lances pinned to the other. He wore a necklace on a silver chain, with a heavy skull hanging from the end, a lance through one empty eye socket. Even out of his armor he seemed unbelievably big, not a quarter shy of seven feet tall with arms that could choke a swamp dragon.

Devan made a strangled sound in the back of his throat and removed his hands from Taniel's jacket. "They have to wait in line just like everyone else. The Lady Chancellor's orders."

Styke put one hand on Devan's shoulder, squeezing until he elicited a gasp. "Lindet sent me out into that stinking swamp to find them. You think I'd put up with that shit if it wasn't important?"

They were ushered inside without further argument and soon found themselves in the chapel vestibule. The thick church doors managed to suppress the noise of the outside crowd to a low hum, and the inside was pleasantly devoid of the jostling crowds. A few small groups, no larger than a dozen in each, conferred quietly throughout the chapel. Taniel could hear their nervous titter as he entered and saw their expectant glances toward the front of the room.

Styke marched Taniel and Ka-poel up to where the altar had been replaced by a wide, wooden desk. It was covered in maps, messages, and papers, not unlike the desk of Taniel's father back home.

Lindet was a woman with soft, round features and blond hair a few shades lighter than Styke's. She looked up, and Taniel was immediately taken by her eyes. They were blue like the sky on a clear sunny day, and had the fire of ambition in them that he saw in young officers ready to prove themselves by charging into the face of enemy grapeshot. There was a flicker of interest as her gaze passed over him, pausing on Ka-poel, and then moving on to Styke. Taniel was shocked at how young she was—twenty-three or twenty-four, perhaps. She was not tall, nor particularly striking, and she might be mistaken for a mild-mannered librarian if you came across her in the street. But her eyes...

This was the Fatrastan governor who'd spearheaded the revolution against Kez?

"Lindet," Styke said, interrupting the narrow-faced man whispering in Lindet's ear.

Lindet held up one finger, waiting until the messenger had finished, then dismissed him with a wave. He fled to a smaller desk in the corner of the room. "Styke." She spat the name, glancing at Taniel and his companions as if they were supplies being delivered on her doorstep. "You bring me the Tristan Ghost Irregulars?"

"That's us, ma'am," Taniel said.

Lindet pursed her lips. "Who's the Palo?"

"Local girl," Taniel answered. "She's my guide and spotter."

Ka-poel crossed her arms, scowling at him. He did his best to ignore her.

"And you're Two-shot?" Lindet asked. Her eyes bore into him, studying him as thoroughly as he might inspect his rifle before a fight.

It was a rhetorical question, but he answered anyway. "Yes, ma'am."

"I've heard good things about you," she said, without any of the warmth that usually accompanied such a statement. "If I had a hundred of you, the war would be long over. But I don't. Tell me, do you think your father would support an Adran alliance with Fatrasta against the Kez?"

Taniel was immediately taken aback by the question. "I wouldn't presume to speak for him. But it's uh, probably not a good time. He's focused on domestic issues."

"I see." She leaned forward slightly, her study of Taniel's face intensifying, before tilting her head slightly as if to look over her shoulder. The narrow-faced man quickly rushed to her side. "I've made my decision," she told him. "Get me Petrov and je Stoy. And those fools over there. They'll want to know as well."

What decision? Taniel shot a worried glance at Ka-poel, but the girl seemed pensive, all her attention on Lindet like a mongoose watching a snake. Styke stood with his hands clasped behind his back, looking mildly interested in the proceedings as the messenger slipped out through the back of the church.

"If you don't mind me asking, ma'am," Taniel said, "you summoned us here in an emergency. Do you have an assignment for us?"

"Patience, Two-shot," Lindet said. "You'll have killing to do before the week is out. But circumstances have changed since I sent Styke to look for you."

Styke perked up. "What's changed? Do we have more reinforcements?"

"No," Lindet said. "That's the problem. We've got barely three thousand fighters here. They range from skirmishers to infantry to suicidal madmen." She flicked an annoyed glance at Styke, who grinned back at her. "We have a single Privileged of our own, who can't hope to match the four the Kez have sent."

"Three," Taniel said. "I killed one."

"Three the Kez have sent." Lindet made a note and continued as if he hadn't spoken. "I like Planth. It's well protected inside the Tristan Basin, fairly inaccessible to the Kez armies but with a good enough highway that I can send messengers in and out at speed. My original plan, when I heard the Kez had sent an army, was to defend the city so it would remain my seat of power." She paused, pursed her lips, and continued, "I *was* going to have the Ghost Irregulars lead four hundred skirmishers to harry the Kez flank as they approached the city. Our infantry to meet theirs in open battle, and our cavalry to hit their other flank. But that won't work any more."

"We don't have enough men?" Taniel guessed.

"We don't have enough men," Lindet confirmed.

"What about the reinforcements from Redstone?" Styke asked.

"They're not coming," Lindet replied, her voice dripping with acid. "They claim they have their own problems, and if Redstone isn't under considerable duress when I arrive, I'll drag the garrison commander in front of a firing squad. Without help from Redstone, we can't hope to hold out here."

"What, may I ask, is our next step, ma'am?" Taniel asked.

The narrow-faced messenger appeared from the back of the church, leading a small procession of administrators dressed in fine suits and top hats. They bowed and scraped before Lindet, though the expression on her face said she'd rather they not, and once a few more of individuals had joined them Lindet answered Taniel's question.

"We're retreating," she announced.

"You mean like I said you should have a week ago?" Styke asked.

There was an audible silence following the remark. Someone swallowed loudly. Taniel got the distinct impression that not many people got away with talking back to Lindet.

"Yes," she finally said. "Exactly like that."

"Good."

"Kuskan," she called to her messenger. "Pack everything. But do it quietly. I don't want to cause a panic." She turned her attention back to her administrators. "We're going to withdraw under cover of darkness and take the Basin Highway up to the Cypress Road, where we'll cut across toward Redstone. We'll regroup there and assess our losses."

Taniel frowned. It made sense, of course. The government was too important to stand behind such a risky battle. They *should* run. But once Lindet and her camp pulled out, it left behind a vulnerable city in the path of a Kez brigade. The Kez were not kind to cities that harbored revolutionaries.

"What about the people?" Taniel asked.

"Once we are safely out of Planth, the order will be given to evacuate the city."

"We have two days until the Kez arrive," Taniel protested. "That's not enough time to empty a city of this size, especially if you don't even tell them until tomorrow."

Lindet's gaze fell on Taniel and his throat went instantly dry. He felt more than a little foolish for the fact, wondering what his father, a man who'd told *kings* to piss off, would say about him cowing before a chancellor not even halfway through her twenties.

"The people," Lindet said coldly, "will provide a valuable distraction. Once we've withdrawn and given the evacuation order, people will panic and flee north along the highway. We'll leave behind a defense, of course—you and your

Ghost Irregulars, some of the soldiers and militia—who will harry the Kez just enough to slow them down. Once the government is safely out of harm, you will withdraw."

Taniel felt sick to his stomach. Beside him, Ka-poel bristled like an angry cat. "You expect us to withdraw, leaving ten thousand Fatrastan citizens on the highway, weighed down with all their possessions, at the mercy of a Kez brigade?"

"Yes. I expect exactly that. I will not waste such valuable assets defending an unimportant city."

All around the room, heads nodded thoughtfully as if Lindet spoke the kind of wisdom they expected from their leader. Only Styke seemed at all unsure. "Two-shot is right. They'll slaughter everyone who tries to run."

"And anyone who bothers to stay," Lindet said. "We can't win. At least this way, we'll be able to fight another day with little risk to the government or our field assets. If we'd withdrawn earlier we might have avoided this path, but what is done is done."

Taniel searched Lindet's face for any sign of regret, or perhaps remorse at the idea of leaving a whole city to die. Her eyes were hard, unyielding. She had made her decision and would not bend.

Pit, he realized. His father would probably *like* her.

"No word of our conversation leaves this room," Lindet announced. "There will no doubt be a tragic slaughter once we've gone, and our people can turn it to propaganda to help our cause. These lives won't be wasted. Two-shot, I expect you to prepare your Ghost Irregulars for combat. And you, Styke, keep your Mad Lancers out of trouble until I need you."

Lindet's tone made it clear that her words were final. With a knot in his stomach, Taniel found himself ushered out of the church and out into the city square, where the crowd seemed even more unruly than when he'd entered.

All these people, he realized, would be dead by the end of

the week.

Taniel stormed through the street, Ka-poel sprinting to keep up, until he saw a boy sitting on the stoop, left leg missing from the knee down, cap out on the ground in front of him. Taniel dug through his kit until he found a few krana coins and tossed them in the cap.

"This city have a newspaper?" he asked.

The boy retrieved his cap excitedly, shaking the coins into his hand and stowing them in a pocket. "Yes, sir," he said. "Three of them, actually. Thank you, sir."

"Which one's the biggest?"

"The Planth Caller, sir."

"Where can I find them?"

"The corner of Main and Manhouch. Just keep going two more streets and take a left. Big red sign. You can't miss it."

"Thanks."

Taniel paused for a moment, eying the direction the boy had indicated, then glanced over his shoulder for any of those thugs he'd seen outside Lindet's headquarters. No one stood out from the crowd. It would be an easy thing, informing the newspaper of Lindet's plans. Word would circulate within a few hours, and people would start leaving immediately. Some of them might even have a chance of outrunning the Kez soldiers.

Ka-poel laid a hand on his shoulder.

"What do you want?" he asked.

Ka-poel scowled at him and shook her head. She pointed at the boy he'd just asked for directions, then cupped a hand over her ear. *I heard that.*

"So?" he asked.

She rolled her eyes and pulled him toward the nearest alley. Once they'd gotten out of the crowd, she turned on him, gesturing so quickly that he couldn't follow any of it.

Taniel glanced toward the crowd, impatient. He needed to get to the newspaper. The sooner people knew what was happening, the better. "Pole! Slow down. What is it?"

She pointed at him, then mimed a hangman's noose. *You're going to get yourself killed.*

"What do you mean?" he asked, playing dumb. He knew exactly what she meant.

Ka-poel mimicked a crown on her head, then pointed at him and mimed the hangman's noose again.

"I'm not scared of Lindet."

She made a book out of her hands.

"Yes, I've heard the stories about her. And they're just that: stories." Everyone had heard the stories about Lindet; that people had disappeared after insulting her, that she'd had officers quietly executed for disobedience. He'd always passed them off as Kez propaganda. Even now, knowing she would abandon Planth without a second thought, he didn't believe the more fanciful tales of her wrath.

But they did give him pause. "All right," he admitted, "There will be reprisal for disobeying her orders. But you don't know my father's reputation. What's she going to do to the son of the Adran field marshal?" The idea of hiding behind his father made his stomach turn, but some things were more important than pride.

Ka-poel didn't look as if she believed that. She punched him in the shoulder, shaking her head and pointing to herself and then making a circular motion.

"What do you mean, *what will happen to you?*" Taniel frowned. "If she kills me, you'll just go back to your tribe. No one will come after you."

Ka-poel snorted and punched him again.

"Ow! Look, Pole, somebody has to do this and it's not going to be anyone in her inner circle. She's going to get all of these people killed."

She pointed at him, then made a circular gesture and

mimed a pistol going off next to her head.

"How am *I* going to get them killed?"

She threw her hands up, making a panicked face and running back and forth from one wall of the alley to another. She stopped, pointing at him, miming a hangman's noose. Then the crown again, and a handing-over motion.

It took Taniel a few moments to work out what, exactly, she meant. "You think I'll cause a panic, get myself court-martialed, and maybe even hand Lindet over to the Kez?"

Yes.

Taniel paced the alley, trying to force himself to calm down. He was furious that Lindet would leave so many people to die to screen her own escape. It was something no good Adran soldier would stomach, and Taniel's father was known all over the world for his merciless tactics. But Ka-poel had a point. Lindet's strategy was the only one available to them if they were going to make the most of this mess.

Lindet should have left the moment she heard the Kez were coming for her. She should have evacuated the city with the very next breath. But there was nothing Taniel could do about any of that now. "Half these people won't even leave," he admitted out loud. "They've built houses, planted farms, started families. Settlers that have come as far out as Planth did so because they don't have anything else. This is their home."

Ka-poel nodded in agreement. She squatted, making a quick sketch in the mud of the alley floor. It was a square with smaller squares at each of the corners. A fort. She pointed at it, then firmly at the ground.

"You think the garrison will remain?" Taniel asked.

She nodded again.

He mused over that thought. Frontier garrisons like the one in Planth were often permanent fixtures, their members raised from the local militia, giving them more reason to stay and defend the city in the case of an organized attack by hostile Palo or a local warlord. Ka-poel was right. They'd stay even if Lindet ordered them out of the city.

Taniel found a crate to sit on, putting his chin on his fist and staring out at the passing traffic. "The garrison has five hundred men," he said. "Even assuming none of them run, they'll be slaughtered by the Kez brigade and their Privileged."

Ka-poel pointed at him then mimed firing a rifle.

"I don't know if I can kill the Kez Privileged before they come within range of the city. Besides, even if I take out their Privileged that's still five thousand infantry and auxiliaries. You think I can handle all that myself?"

Ka-poel rolled her eyes. She made a creeping motion with one hand, the signal she used to indicate the Tristan Ghost Irregulars.

"There's less than three hundred of us," Taniel said.

Ka-poel mouthed the words, *then get help*.

Taniel sighed, shaking his head. He had a great fondness for Ka-poel. She was clever, dangerous, and funny. She was an outcast from her own tribe, the way he felt so often among other soldiers. But she didn't understand large-scale logistics. Even if he managed to convince a half dozen militias to stay and help fight the Kez, it was a losing battle—the whole reason Lindet was retreating in the first place.

"There's got to be another option," he said. He sat thinking for several minutes before the very beginning of a plan began to form in his head. It was reckless, but it was better than letting Planth burn just so Lindet could escape.

But Ka-poel was right. He would need help.

Taniel sent Ka-poel with a note for Bertreau and then went through the city on his own, asking for directions until he got the information he wanted: the Mad Lancers were camped on the far side of Planth where their horses could take advantage of a pair of fields for fresh grazing.

Traffic between the lancers' camp and Planth was sparse, and there was a wide berth between them and the closest militia camp. Taniel had heard stories about the Mad Lancers; suicidal charges, flouting orders, whole towns full of Kez sympathizers put to the torch. They sounded like a commanding officer's worst nightmare and only their reputation for saving lost battles and coming to the aid of the common people had managed to associate their name with an admiring word rather than a curse.

Rumor had it that even the regular army avoided them.

Taniel approached their camp cautiously and was more than a little surprised to find a proper guard circling the perimeter in regular intervals. There were two men and a woman, all three of them wearing the same yellow cavalry jackets as their colonel. They stopped Taniel with a barked command, carbines lowered.

"I'm here to see Colonel Styke," Taniel said, raising his hands.

The woman, taller than the two men by over a hand—nearly as tall as Styke himself—gave Taniel a looking over. "Who are you?" she asked.

"Captain Taniel Two-shot."

"The Tristan Ghost Irregulars?"

"That's me."

The woman lowered her carbine and her two companions did the same. "Major Ibana ja Fles," she introduced herself. "What business do you have with Ben?"

"Just hoping to talk," Taniel said. He wondered at the suspicion in the major's voice. He glanced her over, noting the sword at her side. Her name implied she had some Kez noble blood in her, but more than a few colonial Kez had defected at the beginning of the war. "We're all friends here, aren't we?"

"Some of us more than others," Ibana replied. "Come with me." She nodded for the two men to continue their circuit and fell in beside Taniel, walking them toward the camp before breaking the momentary silence. "Ben says you're a good hand with a rifle."

"It's what I was trained for."

Ibana nodded approvingly. "Heard you've spent almost the entire war holed up in the swamps, raiding Kez supplies. That true?"

"It is."

"Good," Ibana glanced around, lowering her voice. "That means you haven't gotten involved with the politics of this war. Word to the wise—*don't* get involved. And trust Lindet as far as you can throw her."

Taniel snorted.

"Something funny, Two-shot?"

"Sorry, major. Just that Colonel Styke seems pretty friendly with her."

"Friendly? That's a laugh. Lindet puts up with Ben because we've won her a handful of battles that she should have lost. Ben puts up with her because… pit, I don't know why Ben puts up with her. Let's just say there's no love lost and this is one of the few times they've actually crossed paths."

"Fair enough," Taniel said, feeling suddenly out of his depth. He tried to stay as far away from politics as possible—that was his father's realm. He didn't know enough to grasp the nuances of the situation, nor to argue with Ibana's advice. As far as he could see, Lindet was in charge of everything around here. People respected, admired, or feared her and that kept the revolution going. He shook his head. He didn't need to get any more involved. He was just here to fight the Kez and, in this situation, try to save Planth.

Ibana led him to a series of small tents clustered around a campfire. Half a dozen marsh hares roasted on a spit, and just as many soldiers lounged around on camp stools or bedrolls. They were an odd lot—men and women, including a boy of fourteen and a woman well into her sixties. Half of them wore cavalry jackets, two wore buckskins, and a third wore a faded old suit jacket that probably originally cost two months of a cavalryman's wages.

"This here is the company officers," Ibana said. "Little Gamble, Steffan je Lent, Chraston, Sunnintiel, Ferlisia, and the kid is our bugalist, Jack. Everyone, this is Taniel Two-shot."

"Two-shot?" the old woman asked, craning her head as if her hearing wasn't that good. "The powder mage? What's Ben have to say about having another genuine hero in the city?"

"Shut up, Sunnin," Ibana said. "Where's Ben?"

"He went to have a talk with the Blackhats. Should be back any minute."

Ibana swore under her breath. "You let him deal with those thugs by himself? What's wrong with you fools?"

"It's fine, Ibana." Styke emerged from the tents, his cavalry jacket thrown over one shoulder and the biggest knife Taniel had ever seen strapped to his belt. The side of his face was caked with blood, but no one around the fire seemed all that surprised. "Just had to sort some things out with our friends in town."

"What happened?" Ibana asked, pointing to the gash over his eye.

Styke frowned at her, then touched his fingers to his forehead and rubbed the blood between his thumb and forefinger. "Huh. Must have hit me with something. The talking went south. I had to teach Devan a little respect."

Ibana tensed. "Trouble?"

"Nah. He and his friends were off-duty. I think we understand each other now."

Taniel grimaced at the blood. It looked like Styke had been bashed across the head with a millstone, but he seemed no worse for the wear. "Who are the Blackhats?" he asked.

"Two-shot," Styke grunted. "Didn't expect you here. The

Blackhats are Lindet's hatchetmen. They're the ones with the vests and bowler caps you saw in Planth. Thugs and spies, the lot of them, but they're good at their job. Surprised Ibana let you in the camp. Thought I gave orders to keep things tight around here."

"Go to the pit," Ibana responded. "You want me to break your nose again?"

Styke laughed. Taniel looked between them, wondering what kind of an officer relationship this was. That kind of language would end you up on latrine duty for a month, even if you *were* friendly with your commanding officer.

He cleared his throat. "Was hoping to talk with you. In private."

"Yeah? Sure, we can do that."

Styke led them through the camp, over to the impromptu corral the Mad Lancers had built. He pulled a carrot out of his pocket, feeding the first horse to come nuzzle him, and patting it gently on the flank. It was an oddly gentle gesture for a man with such a brutal reputation.

"What do you need, Two-shot?" he asked.

Taniel looked up at the afternoon sun, suddenly feeling like he didn't know where to start. His anger with Lindet had faded, and he wanted to just head off to find the Ghost Irregulars and get some rest. He realized that he hadn't slept much for days, and not at all since yesterday morning.

"This might seem a little strange," he said. "You don't know me, and I don't know you, except by reputation. But I need help."

Styke removed his big knife from its sheath, scowling at it and rubbing some blood out of the groove with his thumb. "What kind of help?"

"You heard Lindet's plans this afternoon. She means to abandon the city to the Kez in order to make her escape and she wants *us* to provide a screen and then withdraw ourselves. I assume she doesn't want to lose any of her local assets protecting a doomed city, but I don't think it's doomed."

Styke stared at him.

Taniel cleared his throat and continued. "The garrison will stay behind, assuming they're local. Two days isn't enough time for the rest of the city to evacuate but I'm thinking about...stretching the terms of my orders and sticking around a bit longer. Maybe trying to buy the people who want to leave enough time to get out of reach of the Kez. I wondered if you'd be interested in doing the same."

"Huh," Styke grunted. He pointed his knife at Taniel. "You're going to stretch *your* orders."

"What do you mean?"

"Lindet is only leaving skirmishers behind. She's sending everyone else to wherever they're needed. The Mad Lancers are supposed to head north, then east to deal with Kez cuirassiers cutting up the countryside a hundred miles from here."

Taniel swore to himself. Why hadn't he thought of that? Of course Styke wouldn't be participating in the delaying action. The Mad Lancers were heavy cavalry—as heavy as you get. If they engaged the Kez, they wouldn't be un-engaging until the battle was over.

"I see," he said. "Yeah, that makes sense. Well, thanks for your time." He turned away, angry that he'd wasted an hour on a fruitless pursuit. Maybe he'd reconsider his idea of heading to the newspaper, without Ka-poel to stop him.

"Hold up," Styke said.

Taniel turned back. Styke was idly picking his teeth with the tip of his knife. "Just out of curiosity," he said, "why'd you come to me?"

Taniel considered the question. "I've spent the last twelve months shooting Kez out in the swamp. I've got a name, I guess, but I don't know anyone. Don't know the politics here. You're the most senior officer I've met. Back with Lindet, you seemed like the only person vaguely bothered that she's leaving Planth to burn. Everyone knows your name, and everyone knows you fight lost causes. I thought you'd be willing to help. Or at least try to convince Lindet to extend the delaying action."

Styke chuckled. "You're right you don't know the politics. Lindet isn't the type to be convinced by anyone. You're either with her or you're against her, and there's very little in between. You might be able to get away with extending your delaying action. But us sticking around? She wouldn't like that at all."

Taniel smiled, kicking himself inwardly. "I don't think I know you enough to ask you to outright disobey orders."

"Probably not," Styke conceded. "Do me a favor, though. Tell me why you're here."

Taniel frowned. "To defend Planth."

"Not here, here. In Fatrasta. What are you? Nineteen? Twenty? You're the son of the most decorated war hero in the Nine. Why are you an ocean away from home, creeping around the swamps, instead of whoring your way through a university in the Nine?"

"It's… " Taniel began. "It's personal."

Styke shrugged. "Everything's personal, Two-shot."

Taniel hesitated for a moment. He didn't like to talk about his father, or about much of anything regarding home. It always sounded too much like whining. But Styke was good enough to give him a few moments of his time. He deserved an honest answer.

"My father sent me abroad to widen my worldview," he said. "I didn't want to go, and he forced it. Sent me away from my friends, my fiancée—everything I knew. I'm not even sure what I was being punished for, but it was definitely a punishment of some kind. Anyways, I managed two weeks of a tour of the Fatrastan coast before the revolution started. I had an excuse to head home, but the Kez killed my mother when I was a boy, so I signed up to shoot at them. I figured it was something that would make my father proud and piss him off all at once."

Styke rolled his tongue around in his cheek, and Taniel could tell he was trying not to laugh. But his grin was companionable, and Taniel found it hard to take offense. "Impertinence, stubbornness, and vengeance all rolled into one," Styke said. "I like it. It has flavor. So what's your plan to defend Planth?"

Taniel didn't dare to hope Styke would offer his help. But Styke was an experienced cavalryman and he'd won more real battles than Taniel had ever fought. Any advice of his would be warmly welcomed.

"Delays," he said. "Not everyone will be willing—or able—to leave Planth but if we can give the rest an extra day or two it might save thousands of lives. I'll start by killing their other three Privileged and then we'll bluff, bargain, and fight until the very last moment."

"And you expect to pull out of it alive?"

"If anyone can, it'll be the Tristan Ghost Irregulars," Taniel said. Of that, he was confident. Of the plan itself… "But if we can't, defending a helpless city isn't a bad way to die."

"You're not the commanding officer of the Ghost Irregulars," Styke pointed out. "Is your Major Bertreau on board with this?"

"She doesn't care much for politics. She likes to fight lost causes, so it won't be hard to bring her around."

"My kind of woman." Styke grinned, an expression that split his broad face in two. "I like you, Two-shot. You've got balls. Come here, let me show you something." Taniel followed Styke back into the camp, where Styke pointed at one of the officers that Ibana had introduced earlier. "That's Little Gamble," he said. "He's a total coward. Hasn't lifted a weapon his whole life. We found him next to the graves of his wife and daughters after a Kez patrol swept through and he's been our quartermaster and banner man ever since."

"The old woman next to him, Sunnin, she buried seven sons after the Kez burned Little Starland to the ground. You wouldn't know it from looking at her but she can aim a lance better than I can. Chraston's farm was torched. Jack's parents were hung for trying to defend their own cattle."

"The story is the same all around here. Everyone fighting the Kez has lost someone close but here, in the Mad Lancers, we take the very worst of them. We take the beaten and broken, the ones without anyone left, the ones who no one believes can fight, and we teach them to ride, to fight, to kill."

"I've got three hundred lances under my command. We've buried at least that many along the way, and every one of them has ridden through the gates of the pit with the wind in their hair, a beloved name on their lips, and a Kez spine pinioned to the end of their lance."

Stunned, Taniel turned to Styke. He'd heard the stories of the Mad Lancers just like everyone else. But he'd had no idea. He opened his mouth, not sure what to say.

"We're the chaff," Styke said. "Lindet doesn't give a damn about our lives and we don't give a damn about her orders. If you want to stay behind and protect Planth, you bet the medals on your daddy's jacket the Mad Lancers will stay with you." He reached out, clasping Taniel's hand.

Taniel could do nothing but clasp back.

Taniel started awake in the darkness, sitting up in his bedroll with sweat rolling down the back of his neck. He remained still for several moments, trying to orient his foggy mind, before seeing a shape at the entrance to his tent.

"Pole?" he asked.

The figure nodded. Or at least, he thought it nodded. He reached for his kit and found an old snuff tin, tapping a line of black powder on the back of his hand. One quick snort later, and his night-vision improved ten-fold as the powder trance kicked in. He could see Ka-poel kneeling at the flap of his tent and behind her, someone else.

"What is it, Pole?"

"Get out here, Two-shot," a voice called gruffly. "The Lady Chancellor wants to see you."

Ka-poel jerked her thumb over her shoulder as if to say *that*. Taniel stiffened. What could Lindet possibly want at this hour? He dressed quickly, tucking a knife into his belt and taking an extra hit of powder as a precaution before climbing out of his tent and finding four of Lindet's thugs gathered just outside. What had Styke called them again? Blackhats.

This didn't look like a social call.

What was going on? Did Styke betray him, telling Lindet about Taniel's plans to keep the Ghost Irregulars behind longer than planned? He almost grabbed his rifle but thought better of it. Nothing was going to happen, he reassured himself. Maybe this *was* just a social call—a last series of orders before she made her escape.

Of course, they wouldn't send four men to bring him in if that was the case.

Taniel accompanied the Blackhats through the militia camp and into Planth, passing the city center until they reached the point at which the highway left the northern part of the city. Taniel expected a wagon train waiting to move Lindet's government on to her next hiding spot and was surprised to see less than a hundred mounted riders waiting beside the road. No carts, no carriages.

Taniel could sense Lindet's lone Privileged among the group and recognized some of the faces he'd seen in the church the day before, both administrators and Blackhats. The former had heavy saddlebags, while the latter were armed with blunderbusses and carbines. Lindet, it seemed, packed light. No wonder she'd managed to stay ahead of the Kez all this time.

Taniel was directed toward the middle of the column, where he found Lindet standing next to her horse, giving quiet directions to one of her footmen. She was wrapped in a cloak despite the warmth, and she seemed small and unimposing to him at first glance. But when she turned those eyes upon him, fiery and critical, he had to keep himself from taking a step back.

"Two-shot," she greeted him.

"Lady Chancellor."

Taniel clasped his hands behind his back, falling into an at-ease position. It was instinctual for a soldier like him, but it also let him keep one hand near his belt knife. He could *feel* the Blackhats still lurking behind him.

"Let's do each other a favor," Lindet said, her tone almost pleasant. "You're not going to pretend that you haven't been plotting to disobey my orders. In return, I'm not going to pretend that your life means even the slightest bit to me. Does that seem fair?"

"I didn't know we were pretending either of those things," Taniel said. "Though I am curious how you knew. Did Styke tell you?"

"Styke didn't have to tell me anything. It's in his nature to disobey me and I half-expected it in this case, even if I did give him a juicy assignment up north. The man's a prat and will one day go too far. But you... I expected better from you, considering your father."

She seemed less like an angry officer and more like a schoolteacher lecturing a wayward youth. Taniel felt suddenly angry. He was a foreigner. A volunteer in this war. He could abandon his post and head home right now, never to return, and no one in Adro would think less of him for it. She should be begging for his help, asking for his council, and instead Taniel got... this.

"You never answered my question," Taniel said.

"Your new friend Styke thought he was quietly asking

around for some extra support in your planned mutiny. He's not as subtle as he thinks. In fact, I don't think Ben Styke has done anything subtle his entire life." Lindet shook her head, a disgusted sneer on her lips.

"I wouldn't call it a mutiny," Taniel said. He focused on his breathing, on keeping calm. What had his father said about dealing with angry superior officers? Smile, nod, and apologize. Well, Taniel damn well wasn't going to apologize. "I simply plan on stretching my orders a bit. Sticking around a little longer than planned to allow more of the Planth citizens to escape."

"Stretching orders," Lindet repeated sarcastically. "You're walking a thin line, Two-shot, but you're right. If you planned outright sedition you'd be in a noose right now."

And I wonder how you'd explain my death to my father, Taniel wondered idly. *You would not like how he reacts to the death of a family member, even if he doesn't seem to think much of me.* Out loud he said, "You didn't have a problem with my disobedience when the Ghost Irregulars risked our necks to delay the Kez advance."

"Because," Lindet replied, her tone gaining an edge of impatience, "the Tristan Ghost Irregulars have been following the same orders for twelve months; to harass and hinder the enemy. I chose to believe you'd never received my latest orders and were simply continuing as you always had."

It was a piss-thin excuse and they both knew it. But Lindet was making it clear she would justify anything she wanted. "And now?" Taniel asked.

Lindet regarded him thoughtfully, looking over his shoulder at the Blackhats standing behind him. Taniel's fingers twitched toward his knife, and he felt himself tense. "My order stands," she finally said. "The Ghost Irregulars are to remain in Planth for the next two days until the Kez arrive, at which time you will provide a delaying action for their advance through the city and up the highway for the next twenty miles. From there you will split off and return to your post in the Basin.

"You can't win," she continued. "The Kez have too many men. Extending your delaying action is very likely to get you and the rest of the Ghost Irregulars killed. You've been a valuable asset in this part of the country, and I will be annoyed at the loss. But I already have one Ben Styke and I don't need another one, so if you decide to disobey my orders I'll see it as a personal favor if you die heroically."

Taniel pursed his lips. Lindet's imperiousness reminded him of an Adran noble, from the way she lifted her chin to the expectation of immediate obedience. But there was a dangerous competence behind her stiff demeanor that reminded him also of his father—something pragmatic and *very* un–noble-like. "Is that all?" he asked.

Lindet took a step closer to him. Taniel was running a strong powder trance. He could kill her before any of her Blackhats could react, and maybe even get away in the chaos but he still felt like *he* was the one who should be cautious.

"If you do manage to survive," Lindet said quietly, "And to save a few thousand Planth citizens, I will pin a medal on your chest when I win this war. But know this: I will remember this insubordination forever. Accidents happen, Two-shot. Even to powder mages."

Taniel noted the way she said *when* she won the war, not *if*. She truly believed she couldn't lose, and Taniel found himself believing as well.

"I'll remember too," he replied. "I'll remember that you're the type of person to abandon ten thousand people to die in order to play it safe."

Lindet pulled herself onto her horse, tugging the reins expertly to wheel around Taniel several times, looking down on him. "I should warn you. My spies tell me that the Privileged have several Wardens with them. Good luck, Two-shot. And be wary. Don't think you can trust Styke. He is a mad dog without a leash. If you don't get yourself killed, he'll do it for you."

Taniel felt the butt of his rifle kick back into his shoulder. He immediately burned the extra powder in his jacket pocket, *willing* the bullet he'd just fired along its path for far longer than any projectile should have stayed in the air. It traveled a hundred yards, then five, then a thousand, until he let it drop suddenly to slam into a Kez Privileged riding her horse along the highway.

Taniel's aim was slightly off at the end and the bullet took the Privileged in the forehead instead of the left eye. The body jerked back in the saddle, slumping to one side, and her bodyguards erupted into chaos.

Taniel watched just long enough to be sure he'd made a kill before handing his rifle to Ka-poel, who swung it over her back and began to descend through the branches of the cypress. They found their canoe hidden in some nearby reeds and set off through the myriad of river channels, heading south. Ka-poel turned back to him and held up two fingers.

"One down," Taniel agreed. "Two to go."

The swift cracking of a barrage of musket fire echoed through the distant trees, and Taniel turned his head to try and pinpoint the location. It took him a few moments before he decided that no, those weren't muskets. They were rifles. Hrusch rifles. Somewhere north of him the Ghost Irregulars had engaged the Kez.

He and Ka-poel paddled their canoe downriver for almost a mile, hiding in inlets from the occasional Kez patrol, before they stashed it again and headed across the highway. They managed to remain unseen by the few bedraggled, lagging rear wagons of the Kez train and then headed north for a ways before they found a good tree to climb.

Their newest vantage gave them a fantastic view of the

Kez army, snaking its way along the Basin Highway as it approached Planth.

By Taniel's estimate, the Kez vanguard was less than six miles from Planth. They'd slowed considerably as they approached, likely expecting that fierce resistance that Lindet *had* planned for them before she decided to flee. So as not to disappoint them, Bertreau and the Ghost Irregulars had split into two parties and were harassing the vanguard's flanks. On the road, Styke's lancers had discarded their lances and armor in favor of mobility and were keeping the Kez from mounting a proper reconnaissance of the city.

It was a simple ruse, and Taniel hoped that it would gain the people leaving Planth an extra half-day. The real problems would begin once the Kez finally reached the city and discovered how few troops remained to defend it.

Taniel remained in the treetop for almost three hours, watching the Kez army creep forward, both he and Ka-poel keeping a steady eye out for the remaining Privileged. Mid-afternoon came and went and they changed positions, and then after a light supper of jerky and dry corn cakes Ka-poel went to move their canoe up the river.

She returned just as the sun was beginning to touch the treetops to the west, settling in on the branch beside him and shooting him a quizzical look.

"Nothing," he responded. "Even the ranking officers are keeping their heads bloody-well down."

It wasn't difficult to find a Privileged. Taniel could open his Third Eye, looking from this world into a parallel one in which a sorcerous aura surrounded anyone with magical abilities. There were ways, however, that a Privileged could mask their aura and remain undetected for periods of time. Taniel didn't understand it entirely, but knew it wasn't easy. It was a testament to his reputation that these Privileged thought it worth their effort. They weren't taking any chances with the lone powder mage lurking in the swamp.

Such a thought should have cheered him up—Privileged, dealers of death and sorcery, afraid of *him*—but it only annoyed him.

"Just poke your head up so you can die," he whispered, sighting along his rifle and doing another sweep of the camp. Even the Privileged's guards were disguising themselves as ordinary soldiers to stay hidden.

All he could do was hope that one of them made a mistake before the sun set.

"I guess," he said, referring to the Privileged, "that staying hidden means they're not engaging either Styke or the Ghost Irregulars. So that's good?"

Ka-poel pulled a sour face.

"Yeah. They can just wait and kill us all tomorrow when we're defending the city." Taniel swore to himself. His body ached from crouching in the treetops all day. It was a deep ache and was even leaking through the powder trance he kept up so he could watch the enemy movements with the greatest precision. "You haven't seen any Wardens, have you?" he asked.

Ka-poel shook her head.

"Lindet said they had a few." A shiver went down his spine. "I *really* don't want to run into a Warden." He said a quick prayer that Lindet's spies were wrong, but he wasn't going to waste too much hope on the thought. Wardens were sorcery-twisted humans, spawned by the horrid magics of the Kez cabal, and most Kez Privileged kept them nearby. They were fast, incredibly strong, and merciless. Like rabid dogs they knew no fear, and could move so swiftly through the ranks, killing as they went, that they were worth thirty or forty ordinary soldiers on a battlefield.

Tomorrow was not going to be a good day.

"Wait," Taniel said, half to himself. He paused in his long examination of the Kez army and adjusted his aim slightly, looking down the barrel of his rifle. An extra pinch of powder sharpened his eyesight, and he noticed four Kez infantrymen walking in a *very* tight formation around a fifth. All five men's shoulders were touching and none of them were carrying muskets.

Privileged *hated* being too close to gunpowder.

Taniel focused on the infantryman in the middle. A man of medium height, his shako was slightly off-kilter and his uniform seemed quite a bit too big on him. Taniel watched the group march for several minutes, noting the way they lagged behind, how the man in the middle walked slightly bow-legged, like someone who was used to riding horses or in carriages.

Taniel pulled the trigger, burning powder as the crack of the rifle echoed in his ear. He guided the bullet along its path, adjusting for wind, drop, and troop movement, fueling its trajectory with miniscule flares of powder until it blew through the middle soldier's throat, splashing crimson across the tan coats of his companions.

As he fell, Taniel felt the smallest surge of sorcery dispel as the disguise dropped, and he was able to see and sense the Privileged in the Else. Taniel forewent his normal examination of the following chaos and nodded to Ka-poel as he prepared to switch spots.

"Just one to go."

Taniel didn't find the last Privileged until well after midnight. The Kez had made camp less than two miles from the outskirts of Planth and gunshots had stopped hours ago, telling him that the Ghost Irregulars and Mad Lancers had pulled back to get some sleep for the night.

Small scouting parties scoured the swamps around the camp, no doubt looking for Taniel but none of them traveling far enough away from the camp to find any sign of him and Ka-poel. Taniel could easily clear a two-mile shot with the proper line of sight and the Kez had left the trees and were now camping in open farmland.

Ka-poel signaled him by gently tapping him on the back of the hand. He took a sniff of powder and made her repeat her flurry of hand-signals twice before he got the gist of her message and began scanning the very center of the army camp for one particular tent among hundreds of others. He found it quickly, his Third Eye revealing a pastel glow, like the flickering of a candle flame, leaking through the Else.

He smiled to himself, the tension leaving his body immediately as he lined up the shot. This was what the entire plan hinged upon—the death of the last Privileged—and he was going to manage it with enough time to slip back to Planth for a few hours of sleep before morning. He examined the target, watching the light flicker in the Else. The Privileged must have fallen asleep and let his disguise slip.

He would die for that mistake.

Taniel slowly exhaled and squeezed the trigger. He burned powder, counting quietly under his breath. ". . . eight, nine, ten, eleven, twelve…" Through his sorcery, he felt the bullet hit its target. He ignored the discharge of the rifle still echoing in his ears and waited for the flicker of the Else to fade as the Privileged's brains dripped down the side of his tent.

The light didn't fade. Rather, if flared to life and suddenly moved, as if the Privileged had leapt to his feet. A cold sweat broke out on the back of Taniel's neck. The shot had missed. Missed, or…

Taniel knew what had happened almost immediately. The Privileged had let his disguise lag on purpose, surrounding himself with a shield of sorcery. Taniel's bullet had pinged off the shield harmlessly and allowed the Privileged to pinpoint exactly where Taniel was.

"It didn't kill him," Taniel whispered desperately. "We have to move. *Now.*"

He handed Ka-poel his rifle and searched for a handhold,

almost losing his balance. Taniel forced himself to pause, take a deep breath, and descend calmly.

That's when he heard the noise.

It was a snuffling sound, not unlike those he'd heard from pigs searching through countryside streets for leftover morsels. This sound was much louder, however, almost directly below their position. Taniel expected to hear infantry crashing through the underbrush or feel approaching sorcery as the Privileged moved within range to retaliate, but this sound was more terrifying than either of those things.

He exchanged a glance with Ka-poel. Her eyes were wide, attentive, and she seemed to be sniffing the wind like a fox.

"Warden," he whispered.

Ka-poel worked her way onto the end of the branch and leaned out, looking down. She nodded back at him. The snuffling stopped, and the branches trembled as something very heavy ascended the trunk of the cypress.

Ka-poel swung the rifle off her back, swiftly reloading. Taniel, his heart thumping, tossed a powder charge into his mouth whole, crunching the grit between his teeth, swallowing the bitter sulfur as strength coursed through him. With so much powder he could outrun a horse, punch out an ox, or outstrike a snake. But could he kill a Warden?

"Rifle," he said urgently. He caught sight of the creature below him, dark, beady eyes looking up from beneath an overhanging brow. What had once been a human man was now shaped by the sorceries of the Kez cabal into something else—a creature of strength and speed, meant to tear the cabal's enemies limb from limb; a monster created to kill powder mages.

He took the rifle from Ka-poel's outstretched hands and flipped it around, sighting down the barrel, only to find the Warden gone.

He listened desperately, eyes searching the dark tangle of branches below him. The silence seemed to laugh back at him, as if the Warden had disappeared into this air. The realization that he'd gone from hunter to hunted in a handful of heartbeats turned his blood cold.

"Where is he?"

Ka-poel had that fox-like look on her face again, head tilted to one side. She'd lost him, too, and that did not bode well. Taniel searched nearby branches and craned his head. Had the Warden fallen? There was nowhere else it could have gone, unless...

Taniel spun just as the creature emerged from around the thick trunk of the cypress, moving between branches like an ape Taniel had once seen in the Adopest zoo. It was huge, hunched over, towering above him at six and a half feet and coming so quickly he could barely raise his rifle in time.

The barrel of Taniel's rifle flashed, stock bucking in his hands as the shot took the Warden just above the heart. The creature didn't even slow, and Taniel had to fling his rifle to one side, hoping the shoulder strap caught on a nearby branch, before the Warden could grasp it in its big, muscled hands.

The beast lashed out, catching Taniel's shoulder with a glancing blow that threw him off his perch. He fell half a dozen feet before he hit a tree limb, a sharp pain going through his chest. He grabbed a handful of leaves, then a branch to keep him from tumbling further. Stars floated in front of his vision and he pulled himself up onto the branch, trying to focus through the pain.

Above him, Ka-poel squared off against the big creature without an ounce of fear in her. She balanced on the end of the branch, nowhere else to run, and thick, black cuts across the Warden's face attested to her skill with the machete in her hand. The Warden snapped its jaws at her like a wolf, growling angrily, bracing itself for a charge.

It would grab Ka-poel and send them both to their deaths forty feet below.

Desperately, Taniel got to his feet, balancing on the tree limb, and leapt upwards. He grabbed the Warden by the ankle, pulling down with all his weight.

The Warden lost its footing, letting out a yelp as it fell, chest and chin hitting the branch on the way down. Claw-like fingernails scrabbled for a hold and Taniel threw himself against the trunk of the cypress to avoid being grabbed as the creature fell.

The Warden crashed through the lower branches until it hit the thick roots of the cypress far below, its body twisted in an unnatural shape. Taniel's relief was immediately arrested as the creature began to move. *It was still alive.*

It soon began to howl and thrash, trying to right itself, no doubt ready to ascend with all the fury of an animal in pain. Taniel found his rifle tangled in a nearby branch and checked the mechanisms quickly before reloading as fast as he dare.

Grappling with a wounded Warden, even with all his strength and speed, would probably get him killed. He had one shot to finish this.

He secured his foothold and aimed downward.

A Warden, he could hear his father's voice say in his head, *is a creature twisted into madness. Its skin is like leather, bones like iron. Skeletal mutations surround its heart and sorcery will keep it alive long after any other beast would give up the ghost. The surest way to kill it is to penetrate the brain—and to do that takes considerable force.*

Taniel fired a shot, putting an extra charge worth of powder behind his sorcery. He forced the power of the charge inward, to keep the bullet from fragmenting when it hit the Warden's thick skull, then *pushed* with his sorcery. The bullet entered the Wardens head and bounced around inside, turning its brain to porridge. It looked up at Taniel, eyes glazing over with a look of surprise, before slumping over.

The thumping of his own heart transfixed Taniel for several long seconds, until Ka-poel's light touch brought him out of his reverie. She pointed toward the Kez camp.

The Privileged!

Taniel scrambled up several branches, ignoring the pain in his chest, until he gained a new perch. His head spun from the fight, but he had to work through it. No time to change positions, no time to run. He found the Privileged heading toward him on horseback, galloping at full speed with gloved hands raised above his head. Taniel cleared the barrel of his rifle, reloading.

He remembered the trap, the shield of air. The Privileged wasn't even bothering to hide himself—or the shield—this time. He was coming on hard, protected by an invisible wall of sorcery that Taniel's bullets could not pierce.

The wall, however, was only *between* them.

Taniel aimed high, pulling the trigger. He floated the bullet along for over a mile before letting it drop naturally. With its current arc, it would overshoot the Privileged by thirty feet. At the last moment, Taniel burned an extra powder charge, pushing the bullet straight down.

The bullet missed the shield of air, piercing the top of the Privileged's head. Gloved hands dropped, and the Privileged tumbled from his saddle.

Taniel slumped backward, allowing himself a long breath of relief. Ka-poel sat immediately behind him, looking over his shoulder, and without her presence he might have tumbled from his perch. He handed his rifle over his shoulder and, once he'd stopped trembling, began the downward climb.

Taniel and Ka-poel entered Planth in darkness. The outskirts of the city were quiet, with barely any signs of life, but as they drew closer to the center, they found families urgently packing wagons, merchants boarding up their shops, and just as many settlers on stoops, cleaning muskets and blunderbusses in preparation for a last stand.

Planth would not go down without a fight, but Taniel had heard the stories of what happened to Little Starland and a half dozen other cities. It would be a slaughter.

He found Bertreau and Styke had taken over Lindet's headquarters in the chapel. Neither looked like they had gotten much sleep. Bertreau sat behind Lindet's desk, perusing reports from the garrison and attempting to take stock of their situation while Styke lounged nonchalantly on one of the pews.

"Well?" Styke asked, half-turning to watch Taniel approach.

Taniel set his rifle on a pew and sat down next to it, feeling achy and weary. He'd let his powder trance lag in the hope he might catch a few hours of sleep, but was less than optimistic about the prospect. His head, chest, and muscles ached, and he reached for a spare powder charge.

"Three Privileged and a Warden," Taniel said.

"Hah!" Styke barked. "Well done, Two-shot"

Bertreau gave a sigh of relief without looking up from her reports. "Thank Kresimir for that. At least we'll be able to go down fighting instead of in a flash of sorcery." She picked up a piece of paper, reading it silently, before finally looking up. "According to Lindet's reports—which she so kindly left behind—there may be two more Wardens with them."

Styke spat on the floor. "We'll ride them down just like the rest."

"You don't ride down a Warden," Taniel said.

"You can ride down anything if your horse is big enough." Styke leaned toward him. "I have a really big horse."

"You're mad."

"That's what people keep telling me."

Taniel shook his head. *Don't trust Styke*, Lindet had warned. It was folly for any sane person to expect to just *run down* a couple of Wardens. Taniel had barely escaped from that creature in the swamp with his life. Styke's lancers wouldn't have a prayer, enchanted armor or not.

"The evacuation?" Taniel asked.

"There are only two roads out of Planth and the Kez are blocking one of them," Bertreau said. "About three thousand people have managed to leave so far, with that many again trying to get out before the Kez attack."

Taniel put his head in his hands. Sorcery may not be a threat any longer, but steel would finish the job just as well.

Bertreau continued, "Our garrison is eight hundred with volunteers. I've taken command of them, and you'll take the Ghost Irregulars tomorrow as we agreed. All we have to do is try to buy the people another couple of days. Then we'll pull out."

And let everyone else die. Taniel nodded. "All right, I…" his thoughts trailed off, his mind hardly able to focus. He glanced behind him, only to find Ka-poel curled up on the next pew, snoring softly. "I need some rest. So do the both of you."

"I'll rest when I'm dead," Styke replied, grinning to himself.

"Right. I'm sure you'll get your chance soon enough." Taniel took off his jacket and folded it into a pillow, lying down on the hard pew.

"Oh," Bertreau said, glancing sidelong at Styke as if he was a dog that might bite, "the Kez have asked for a parley. Tomorrow at noon."

Taniel was already fading. "Tomorrow at noon," he repeated. *Then the real fight begins.*

"I expect nothing less than the complete and unconditional surrender of Planth."

The Kez general was a little taller than Taniel with haughty shoulders, an arrogant black mustache, a dozen medals on his dress uniform, and a smallsword hanging from his belt. He adopted what Taniel liked to think of as a "portrait" stance, with one leg forward and hands on his hips, head held high like he was waiting for the artist to finish a glorious rendition.

"I'm sorry," Styke said, looking down on the general. "Who are you?"

The Kez general sneered. "My name is General Weslin je Jiffou. And you, I presume, are Ben Styke, the Mad Lancer." If he was intimidated by Styke's size, he was doing a remarkable job hiding it.

"*Colonel* Ben Styke," Styke corrected.

"Yes, yes. Is that the best you have? I will not parley with an animal. I'll speak with the general in charge or with that traitor Lindet."

Styke spread his hands. "I'm all you get, Jiffy. The Lady Chancellor is too busy to deal with you and if you think calling me an animal will get a rise…" He shrugged. "I've been called worse by better."

Jiffou made a face like he was holding in a sneeze—though in this case it was probably an indignant sputter. Taniel examined his eyes, watching for what his father called the "noble madness" —that moment when noble officers lost their temper at small things. But instead of an exclamation or a string of curses, Jiffou forced himself to relax. A slow smile spread across his face as he looked from Styke to Bertreau to Taniel and then back to Styke.

"You can parlay with Two-shot here if you'd like," Styke suggested, jerking a thumb toward Taniel. "He's got the military lineage for it, if not the rank." Taniel cleared his throat, hoping his cheeks didn't redden. He was a marksmen and a soldier—*not* a negotiator. He opened his mouth, but Jiffou beat him to the punch.

"Ah, the infamous Taniel Two-shot. I suppose I should offer you my thanks. Your murder of two of my superior officers has landed me a field promotion. One which I intend to keep once I've handed Lindet's head to the colonial governor." Jiffou's smile broadened. "Lindet sends a mad colonel, a nameless major, and a swamp marksmen out to parley? She must be more desperate than I suspected."

Taniel swallowed. This parley needed to accomplish two very important things: it needed to convince Jiffou that Lindet was still in Planth *and* that the defenders had the upper hand. It appeared he already assumed the former. It was the latter Taniel was worried about. They needed him to hesitate.

"We've called in every militia for a hundred miles," Taniel retorted. "It'll be more than enough to deal with a Kez brigade."

"You speak like you have the might of the famous Adran infantry behind you," Jiffou said. "You don't. You have, at best, a few dozen disorganized militias. I am no fool. Now, let us get this over with. I expect the unconditional surrender of the city and for Lindet to be brought to me in chains."

"Withdraw your men from the borders of the city immediately," Styke replied. "Return to New Adopest and inform the colonial governor that Ben Styke had a lovely time with his daughter at the regional gala two years ago and he looks forward to seeing her again."

Bertreau coughed into her hand, unsuccessfully covering a laugh. Jiffou's eyes narrowed. "Jest if you like," he said. "It won't save your necks from the noose."

We're acting too cavalier, Taniel thought. *Overplaying our hand.*

"You have a city full of civilians there," Jiffou said, spreading his hands. He relaxed his "portrait" stance, as if to say he could be a reasonable man. "My orders are to put the city to the torch, but I have the leniency to spare the city if you hand Lindet and her cabinet over to me at once."

"And the defenders?" Taniel asked.

"You'll be arrested and tried as traitors to the crown, of course."

"Huh," Styke said, "you're not very good at this negotiating thing, are you?"

"What is my alternative? Set the city on fire and let you walk free?"

"That sounds more pleasant to me," Styke said.

"You'd let ten thousand people die for the chance to save your own neck?" Jiffou asked.

"You wouldn't?"

Taniel glanced at the colonel sidelong. The two words were blunt, forceful, and had no sound of a bluff about them. He wondered if Styke had really agreed to defend the city out of a sense of duty. Was he just looking for an impossible fight? Was he suicidal—or would he retreat too early and cost them all their lives?

"What makes you think the Lady Chancellor is even here?" Bertreau asked.

Jiffou responded with a moment of silence, looking past Styke to weigh Bertreau thoughtfully. "Has she fled?" he asked, before answering himself, "No. It's a bit late for that bluff, major. My spies would have informed me."

Taniel glanced at Bertreau. Her face was unreadable, but she had to be thinking the same thing he was: Lindet's Blackhats in Planth had managed to turn or expose every single one of the Kez spies. Impressive.

"Hand over Lindet and her cabinet," Jiffou said, "And I'll tell my superiors that the people of Planth were cooperative and offered no resistance, and that I found no military presence in the city when I arrived."

"You'd let us just... walk away?" Taniel asked.

"I would. If you give me Lindet."

So far, Jiffou hadn't displayed the hallmarks of a Kez officer who'd purchased his commission like all the others. He was confident and in control, without being a total fool. He was willing to ignore orders to fry the bigger fish. But Taniel could see the eagerness in his eyes. Capturing Lindet would end this revolution and make Jiffou's career.

"Give us three days to consider," Styke said.

Jiffou scoffed. "You have an hour."

"There are a large number of militias here," Bertreau pointed out. "To peaceably hand over Lindet we'll have to get the approval of the militia commanders. That will take at least three days."

"Yes, while you wait for reinforcements. I'm familiar with your frontier tricks, major." Jiffou tapped his chin, eying the city. He was no doubt willing to sacrifice his entire brigade for a chance at Lindet—but a bloodless finish would be quite the coup. "I'll give you a day," he said. "That is my final offer."

"Done," Styke responded.

The two parties split, Jiffou returning to his camp with his bodyguards while Taniel walked back toward the city with his companions. As soon as they were out of earshot, Styke made a growling sound in the back of his throat, like a dog eager for a fight.

"I'll try to keep their scouts at bay this evening," he said, "but you've got until noon tomorrow to get as many people out of the city as possible. Make every second count."

Taniel was pulled out of his bed by the distant thunder of artillery. He sat up, blinking the sleep out of his eyes, wondering whether it was a dream before a whistling sound caught his ears. There were a series of loud crashes, far too close for comfort, and then he was up and running, pulling his jacket on as he went. It was barely light, no later than six in the morning.

"Pole! We've got a fight," he shouted, slapping the canvas of her tent as he passed.

Church bells began to ring, and Taniel found Styke's men rousing from the makeshift barracks they'd set up in the city square. Armor clattered as man and horse alike were armed in the ancient plate. Taniel found Styke leaving his tent, hopping along with one arm in his cavalry jacket and his pants around his ankles.

Styke saw Taniel and let out a string of expletives.

"I thought we had until noon?" Taniel shouted above the

whistling of Kez shells.

"Damned Kez must have figured out our game. Bloody pit and bloody damn blasted son of a bitch. You better hope they plan on a good shelling before they send in their infantry because it takes real damned long to get this armor on." Styke gestured to the big warhorse his groom was rubbing down and the ten stone of armor laid out on the ground next to it. "Tell Bertreau to buy us some time."

Bertreau, it seemed, was already ahead of Styke. Taniel arrived at Fort Planth to find the entire garrison already lining up in formation while the fort cannons were aimed and loaded.

Taniel and Ka-poel joined Bertreau on one of the fort lookout towers and stared across the fog-covered field to the Kez camp almost two miles away. At some point during the night their artillery had been moved up—six light mortars and eight guns—and the army were already in formation, waiting for the order to advance.

It took five minutes for Fort Planth's six light cannons to return fire, and only fifteen minutes before one of them had already been slagged by the enemy artillery. The Kez had the weight, range, and numbers on the heavy guns. Taniel returned fire with his rifle when he could, picking off gun crews and mid-ranking officers but it seemed that the Kez had a replacement ready for each soldier he killed.

The field was soon obscured by powder smoke, making his opportunities fewer and farther between.

"Looks like he's just going to sit out there and shell the city," Bertreau said glumly.

"It'll give Styke time to get ready, at least."

Bertreau shot Taniel a look. She pointed at the slagged cannon less than fifty yards from them. "It doesn't matter whether we have Styke or not. If Jiffou shells us until he runs out of ammunition half the city will be on fire and we'll be lucky if there's a garrison left to defend it." She shouted for a messenger to evacuate the remaining civilians from the southern half of the city.

"Would you rather walk out into their grapeshot?" Taniel asked.

"I'd rather," Bertreau said sourly, "they come to us."

Their entire strategy depended on exactly that. If the Kez advanced, the garrison could hold the center, gradually withdrawing through the city while Styke made passing strikes at the enemy's right. Taniel and his Ghost Irregulars already had canoes waiting in the river, allowing them to skirt the enemy left and hit them from behind. But Jiffou, it seemed, was having none of it.

A nearby explosion made Taniel jump, and he turned just in time to see one of the other fort towers take a direct hit from a mortar and topple on its side, sending its occupants tumbling like toys.

Bertreau relocated her vantage point to a chapel bell tower further into the city, though smoke from spreading house fires and spent powder obscured almost the entire battlefield. Taniel squinted into the haze, listening carefully for the sound of snare drums that would indicate the Kez advance.

"They're not coming," Bertreau finally said after nearly two hours of the constant bombardment. The last of the garrison cannons had been destroyed. Nothing opposed the Kez artillery and Taniel had the gut-wrenching feeling, deep down, that Bertreau was right. The Kez would continue their attack from a distance until there was nothing left to fight them.

The garrison hid in the dubious shelter of blasted buildings, their numbers depleted by exploding shot, their faces grim. Taniel could see the doubt in their eyes—only three-quarters remained able-bodied. A few hours ago they were ready to die for their homes and families and now they wondered if they still had time to run. Of the assembled men, only Ka-poel seemed unfazed.

The strike of horseshoes on cobbles approached, and Taniel caught sight of Ben Styke riding along down the street, an imposing figure on his armored warhorse, lance balanced on his stirrup. He stopped below the church, putting up his visor, and called up to them.

"I've had my lancers riding lookout for over an hour. The Kez aren't even trying to flank or cut us off."

"They don't have to," Bertreau replied bitterly. "They'll sift through the ashes of the city in a few days then ride down any survivors."

Styke's horse pranced beneath him, and Taniel wondered how any creature could feel giddy with so much weight on its back. Styke patted its armored neck with one gauntlet. "I'm not going to wait around to die."

"If we retreat, these people die." Bertreau gestured at the city around them, several dozen blocks of which were already in ruins.

"Retreat?" Styke laughed. "Who said anything about retreating?"

Taniel did some quick math in his head. The numbers—and the feeling in his gut—told him that their best chance was still to fight a defensive battle. "If we charge, we're giving up any chance of withdrawal," he said.

"I've got three hundred heavy lancers, Two-shot. My lancers do not withdraw. We're preparing to charge as we speak."

"You'll get cut to ribbons by that artillery!"

"They won't even see what hits them," Styke shot back.

Taniel felt a knot tighten in his stomach. Damn it, Styke *was* suicidal. Styke stared up at him for several moments before lowering his visor and riding back the way he'd come. Taniel thought once again about Lindet's warning. Styke would get them all killed.

And Taniel, he decided suddenly, was going to help him.

"Where the pit is he going?" Bertreau asked.

"He's going to charge the enemy."

"He's going to…" Bertreau trailed off, her attention on soldiers down at the other end of the street, before her head whipped around to face Taniel. "Kresimir above, he's going to what? Three hundred lancers against fifteen times their number in infantry? Is he a bloody idiot?"

Taniel ran down the belfry steps and into the street, after Styke. His heart was hammering in his chest, but he already knew what they had to do before he spoke it. "Pole!" he called over his shoulder. "Check on the Ghost Irregulars. Make sure the canoes are ready."

"Ready for what?" Bertreau demanded, running to keep up with him. "The Ghost Irregulars aren't taking the canoes until the Kez have committed to the city. To do otherwise would leave them sitting ducks."

"Oh, I know," Taniel said. "I'll be with them. Styke! Styke!" He found Styke two streets down, heading toward the city center. "You're going in?" he asked once Styke had wheeled to face him.

"I am," Styke said.

"Major," Taniel said, turning as Bertreau caught up again. "You have to follow him."

"You're as mad as he is!" Bertreau said.

"Maybe," Taniel answered. "But we're never going to have the advantage in this fight. Styke's going to charge no matter what we say, and if you take the garrison in after him we might catch them by surprise."

"Tell me, Two-shot, have you ever surprised anyone to death?" Bertreau demanded.

Taniel grimaced. This was suicide. He knew it, Styke knew it, and he could see in her eyes that Bertreau knew it too. Still, he pressed with a confidence he didn't feel, "If we hit them hard, right up the middle, they might break. If they break, we win—outnumbered or not."

"The Kez infantry are conscripts," he continued. "They're not that much different from us, except they *really* don't want to be here. Their officers are nobility. The infantry know that no matter how hard they fight, they'll never advance the ranks. This makes them particularly susceptible to a rout. Hit them hard enough and they do not bend. They break."

Bertreau's eyes narrowed, and she glanced between Taniel and Styke. "You sound dangerously like your father," she said.

I bet he never did anything quite this stupid, Taniel thought. "Styke will lead through the center. He's the wedge. You and the garrison will drive the wedge home. I'll take the Ghost Irregulars along the far side of the river and come around behind them to cause panic, killing officers as I go. It'll work." *It has to, or we're dead.*

Bertreau eyed Taniel for several moments, then gave a tired nod. "All right, Two-shot. We'll do it your way. You," she said, pointing at Styke, "had better damn well account for yourself before they take you down."

"I'll do my work," Styke said. "Just do yours. And Two-shot, don't kill Jiffou."

"Why not?" Taniel asked. The moment he got a bead on the Kez general, he intended to pull the trigger.

"Because you've made them familiar with the murder of their officers," Styke said. "It's no longer shocking. If you want them to break, truly, you can't just shoot the head. You've got to cut it off, remove the eyes and tongue, and hang it by the hair from the highest branches."

"And how," Taniel asked, "do you intend to do that?"

Styke put his visor back down, and his voice echoed from within. "I'm going to slaughter him and his whole officer corp."

Taniel found Ka-poel waiting at the keelboat docks not far

from Fort Planth, along with almost two hundred and fifty men—a mix of the Ghost Irregulars and their Palo allies. He paused to take stock of the soldiers, worn out from skirmishing with the Kez these last two days, but didn't find a coward among them. There was hesitation in some of their eyes, even fear, but it was accompanied by the stubborn set of the jaw.

The Ghost Irregulars wouldn't run until he gave the order.

Taniel slapped Sergeant Mapel on the back, jumping up on a crate to see the whole group and grabbing Mapel's shoulder for balance. He suddenly felt very young and small, as many of these men were old enough to be his father, but knew that it was more important to show confidence now than ever.

"Slight change of plans," he said. "The Kez won't advance. They think they can hide behind their artillery and blast away all day and that we'll sit on our thumbs and take it. Well, if they won't come to us then we'll go to them." Sergeant Mapel made a sound in the back of his throat. Taniel squeezed his shoulder, silently willing him to keep his peace. He continued, "Colonel Styke's Mad Lancers are heading straight down the center. Major Bertreau will lead the garrison in after him. We're going to take the canoes downriver and hit them from the flank as planned, but we're going to have to row a little harder."

It occurred to Taniel that Bertreau had been given the deadliest job. Styke might be able to ride through and escape if he found an opening, and the Ghost Irregulars could withdraw from the flanks at any time—but there was no escaping for Bertreau. His hackles raised as he realized that he'd probably seen her for the last time, and in his excitement to follow Styke he'd urged her on to her own death.

"Keep it simple, boys," Taniel finished, hearing his voice crack. "And we'll get out of this alive." He got down from crate and said to Mapel in a low voice, "We hug the far bank of the river. We do what we can to draw off a few companies, but if things go south, we disappear into the swamp. Make sure everyone is carrying their full kits."

"What about Bertreau?" Mapel asked.

Taniel considered telling Mapel the truth, but paused, hating himself for it. "She wanted it this way. Final orders." If Bertreau lived through the engagement, Taniel would deal with the lie then. But for now, he didn't need anyone distracted. He felt sick to his stomach.

Mapel nodded and began directing everyone toward their canoes. Taniel joined Ka-poel in the lead canoe and they soon set off, paddling to the opposite riverbank and then holding steady while the rest of the tiny flotilla caught up, then slowly working their way downstream.

Once they were outside the city, visibility improved significantly. A gentle breeze carried powder smoke away from the Kez artillery, allowing Taniel to see the enemy spread out across a slight incline. It gave him a startlingly good view of the battle that caused a brief spike of satisfaction—followed by the realization he'd have a front-row seat to witness Bertreau, the garrison, and the Mad Lancers all die.

Taniel sniffed a pinch of black powder to improve his sight and was quickly able to tell that the Kez had, indeed, already seen him and his Ghost Irregulars. There was waving and shouting, but their attention was quickly drawn away to Planth as the garrison took up position on the outskirts of the city.

The garrison was a motley group, only about half wearing the yellow jackets of the Fatrastan army, but they were well-armed and holding firm. Taniel could see Bertreau leading from the front, shouting orders and curses as she got them all into line. They looked so outnumbered that Taniel almost ordered the Ghost Irregulars to withdraw immediately.

"I don't want to watch this," he muttered.

Ka-poel turned around in her seat and studied his face. She touched two fingers to her eyes and pointed at Planth.

"Yes," Taniel said. "I can see it fine."

She repeated the gesture.

"I'm going to watch, even if I don't want to," he said, his voice rising in anger.

Ka-poel shook her head emphatically and repeated the gesture a third time. Taniel finally decided to ignore her, fixing his eyes on the battlefield while she steered them through the reeds. As he did, he saw the garrison's formation suddenly flex, and then split. What happened next took his breath away.

The Mad Lancers rode through the new gap, four abreast, their steel plate armor glinting in the sun. Their lances were up, streaming yellow banners, and their hooves thundered so loudly across the fields that Taniel could hear them from a distance. They stayed in formation, shoulder-to-shoulder, nose-to-tail with the precision of a crack Adran cavalry unit. Each rider looked like a miniature fortress moving across the battlefield and the whole unit together was simply stunning. He'd never seen anything like this and knew he never would again in a thousand years, wondering briefly how anyone had managed to hold the line against a charge like that in the old days.

But the Kez were a modern military, not medieval yokels with spears. Their artillery crews scrambled to reload, captains no doubt demanding canister shot.

The Mad Lancers took to the field between the Kez and Planth. Their progress seemed impossibly slow as they spread out into a V formation with Styke and his immense warhorse comprising the tip of the spear. Behind them, the garrison fell into step, advancing in their wake at double time.

Taniel barely remembered to lift his rifle to pick off a Kez gunner, reloading it himself as he watched the Mad Lancers. It was a brave charge, a glorious charge. A doomed charge.

They closed within three hundred yards and the Kez cannons belched flame and canister shot like enormous blunderbusses. Taniel turned his eyes on Styke, ready to watch the Mad Lancers fall like wheat before a scythe.

The enchanted armor shrugged off the canister shot like it was nothing more than rain. Taniel heard himself let out a loud cheer as the Mad Lancers charged through the cloud, not a single horse tripping or man falling from his saddle. The Kez gunners panicked, reloading, as their infantry tried to move forward in time to protect them.

It wasn't quick enough. Lances lowered, and the gunners were mowed down, disappearing beneath the armored chests of the horses. A cloud of smoke went up from the front line of infantry as they opened fire. Taniel thought he saw a single rider go down, and then a wall of bayonets presented itself to the Mad Lancers. The armored warhorses smashed through it like it was a garden hedge.

Taniel found his mouth hanging open, and turned to find a smug smile on Ka-poel's face. "How did you know?" he asked.

She tapped one eye, then traced her breast and thumped the middle of her chest—a breastplate. She'd taken a long, hard look at the Mad Lancers' armor, it seemed, and found it more robust than Taniel had guessed. The damned girl hadn't even bothered to tell him.

The Lancers were now entirely encircled, the Kez lines desperately attempting to bring their bayonets to bear. Enchanted armor or no, they were all mortal men and horses. Taniel saw one lancer fall, and then another, and another. Their advance slowed from the weight of the Kez infantry and they soon disappeared in a swirl of bodies and powder smoke.

Certain that no one would emerge from that melee alive, Taniel picked off a Kez major, stopping to reload with two bullets, killing a sergeant and a captain with the next shot, and then watched as the garrison approached the hole Styke had made in the Kez middle.

The garrison stopped, opened fire once, and then charged with bayonets fixed. Their charge was less stylish than Styke's and far less powerful. They slammed into the Kez lines like demons from the pit but were held up almost immediately as Kez officers organized their forces to face them.

The Kez middle bowed, then pulled back as a company broke and ran before the fury of the Planth garrison. The rout caught on in the flanking companies, but went no further as the Kez shored up their defenses and sought to encircle the garrison. Taniel's heart fell. This wasn't going to go well. Not at all.

He watched them fight and watched them fall, firing and reloading as quickly as he could. The barrel of his rifle was hot to the touch, the smell of powder stinging his nostrils, when suddenly his canoe was past the Kez lines. It was the moment he'd been dreading. Would he order the Ghost Irregulars to withdraw or would they commit and hit the Kez from behind?

It hardly seemed like any decision at all after witnessing a charge like that. "Cross the river," he barked, setting down his rifle to help Ka-poel row.

They were on the opposite bank within moments, Ghost Irregulars and Palo leaping from their canoes in the shallow waters and taking to the bank, where they waited until everyone had disembarked. Taniel stood up, rifle raised above his head. They were less than a hundred yards from the Kez rear, and all the Kez focus was on the Mad Lancers and garrison now in their midst.

"Fire!"

They reloaded and fired five more times, Taniel killing any officer that he saw trying to give orders, before the Kez rear lines managed to turn themselves around. It was a chaotic mess, men falling by the score, but Taniel feared it wasn't enough. Three full companies of infantry faced his Ghost Irregulars now, marching toward the riverbank, and he had nowhere to go. They could throw themselves into their canoes and hope to draw those companies further down river.

Or they could stay and be slaughtered with the rest of their allies.

A saying his father had once told him sprang to mind: *A glorious death only comes to two types of people: desperate men with no options, and fools.* The canoes were his option, and Taniel opened his mouth to give the order to withdraw.

His words were swallowed by a cry from further down the bank. He turned his head to see what was happening, only to witness a small group of horsemen emerge from the Kez lines. A sniff of powder and the group came into focus—it was General Jiffou and his bodyguard and they were riding *away* from the battlefield.

The reason for their retreat was almost immediately apparent. A small group of lancers sprang from the melee to give chase. Styke was at their head, his armor smeared with gore, his horse seemingly no more the weary from its charge. At some point Styke had lost his helmet and his lance, and as he galloped after Jiffou he drew his carbine from the saddle and neatly picked off the bodyguard closest to Jiffou.

"By Kresimir," Taniel heard someone say, "The Mad Lancers are still alive."

Taniel looked toward the Kez infantry advancing toward his Ghost Irregulars. "Into the canoes!" he bellowed. "A hundred yards down stream then we're out to fight again. The rear paddles, the front reloads." He scrambled into his canoe, handing his rifle to Ka-poel, and they were off with a shot. He barely watched the water in front of him, his eyes glued to the small drama playing out behind the enemy lines as he paddled hard.

Despite being weighed down with their armor and having just charged through an entire brigade, Styke's lancers closed the gap to Jiffou's bodyguard until Jiffou was forced to turn and fight. The two sets of cavalry smashed into each other with an audible crack, the lancers outnumbered three-to-one.

Taniel threw down his paddle and took his rifle from Kapoel, leveling it at Jiffou. He picked off a bodyguard and continued to reload, only pausing when he noticed another disturbance in the Kez rear line.

Two figures burst into sight, sprinting across the fields after Styke's lancers. They ran hunched over, sometimes on two legs and sometimes on all fours, as swift as horses with long black hair streaming from ugly, misshapen faces. It was the two remaining Wardens that Lindet had warned him about. They would tear Styke apart before he could take down Jiffou.

"Ground us!" Taniel shouted, almost capsizing them as he leapt from the canoe. He waded to shore, climbing up on the bank, and brought his rifle to bear on the first of the running Wardens. The bullet ripped through the creature's jaw, blood spraying its black coat, but it barely seemed to notice the wound as it continued forward.

Taniel swore and began to run, the strength of his powder trance letting him quickly outstrip the Ghost Irregulars that followed him to the bank. He was the only person here—probably the only person in this army—that could go toe-to-toe with a Warden. He wasn't going to allow Styke to do it alone.

He reloaded as he ran, ramming two bullets down the barrel and letting himself pause, taking a deep breath to still his beating heart. Two of Styke's lancers had fallen and most of Jiffou's bodyguards, the last few men desperately trying to protect their general. All Styke needed was a little longer...

Taniel pulled the trigger. He aimed both bullets at the wounded Warden, muttering what his father had told him about shooting the foul creatures: "One for the head, one for the heart."

The bullets struck true. The Warden tripped, stumbled

several more feet and then collapsed, its body twitching several times before growing still. Its companion paused briefly, shooting a glance at Taniel, before charging ahead at Styke.

Taniel desperately tried to reload, but he could already see his fastest wasn't good enough.

The Warden cleared the distance to the lancers and leapt up behind one in the saddle. It jammed a knife through a slit in the lancer's armor, crimson spilling out across the polished steel, and the lancer tumbled from his horse. The Warden made a similar jump, dispatching a second lancer in the same manner in a matter of moments before full-on tackling Styke off his horse.

The pair landed in a jumble, rolling through the mud. The Warden ended up on top, straddling Styke, and its big fist rose and fell, slamming across Styke's unprotected face with the force of a mule's kick.

Taniel finished loading his rifle and lifted it, ready to take the shot, only to see Styke's gauntlet slam into the Warden's chin hard enough to lift it into the air. The Warden wheeled away, stunned, and Styke gained his feet. His face was a bloody mess, lip and brow streaming blood, but he looked nothing like someone who'd just been punched by a Warden.

He just looked angry.

The Warden charged Styke's stomach, driving him back, but Styke did not fall. He wrapped one arm around the Warden's neck and drove the other into the Warden's side again, and again, and again. They grappled for several moments, slipping and sliding through the dew-damp grass before Styke let out a shout and lifted the Warden into the air, twisting the creature's body.

At fifty yards, Taniel heard the snap of bone.

Stunned, he watched as the limp corpse fell out of Styke's arms. Styke shook his head, casting about for his sword, and then saw Taniel. He shouted something, and it took Taniel a moment to realize what it was.

"Shoot the bloody general!"

Taniel raised his rifle, seeing Jiffou retreating back toward the ranks of his army with his last remaining bodyguard. Taniel put a bullet just under his left shoulder-blade and ran toward Styke.

He found the colonel wiping blood off his face with the Warden's jacket, waving down one of his lancers.

"You just killed a Warden *with your bare hands,*" Taniel said. He couldn't hide the shock in his voice. He wanted to tell someone, to tell everyone, never mind the battle still raging around him. A damned Warden!

"He had it coming," Styke said. "Nice shot, by the way."

"It was nothing."

"Not Jiffou—the other Warden. I couldn't have handled two of them. Well done." Styke nodded his head toward the approaching lancer and held something out to Taniel. "Do me a favor and give this to Jack—he's the boy coming up behind you."

Taniel looked down to find a bugle in his hand. "Why?"

"Because that belonged to one of Jiffou's bodyguards," Styke answered, grinning. "And Jack can play their retreat command."

It was raining, and Taniel dug Major Bertreau's grave a mile west of Planth on a hummock among the roots of a big cypress tree. The Ghost Irregulars gathered around, Fatrastans and Palo alike, and six men lowered her to the bottom of the wet hole, her body wrapped tightly in buckskin blankets, her sword clutched in the one hand sticking out of the wrappings.

Taniel said a few words—he couldn't remember after what they were, and he doubted anyone else could either—and then they filled the grave with stones, covered it with soil, and carved her name deep into the flesh of the cypress: *here lies Major Bertreau, died defending Planth from the Kez in K.Y.1521.*

The Ghost Irregulars returned to the city one at a time until only Taniel and Ka-poel remained, rain running off the brims of their hats, clothes soaked through. Taniel found himself thinking of the poor drawing he had of Bertreau in his sketchbook and wishing he'd had the chance to do a better job.

Men died all the time, friends, enemies, and strangers, and Taniel had always felt detached from the fact, as if it was happening in a dream instead of real life. But this seemed different. He'd urged Bertreau into the teeth of the Kez army and she'd died because of it.

"We lost half the garrison the other day," Taniel said, "and I don't give a shit about any of them even though they died in the same fight as Bertreau."

Ka-poel gestured and shook her head. *You didn't know them.*

"I didn't really know Bertreau either," Taniel said. "She wasn't even that good of an officer." *But*, he thought to himself, *perfect for what we needed out here in the swamps.* He kicked a clod of wet soil onto the grave and began walking toward Planth. He emerged from the swamp on the west bank of the Tristan River and paused to gaze upon the city.

Three days had passed since the battle. The fires were all out, bucket brigades aided by a rainstorm that now refused to leave. Some of the fleeing settlers had tentatively returned to the city while others continued to trickle out, worried by the presence of the Kez army still camped a few miles to their south. The city was a wreck, testament to how much damage just a handful of artillery could do in a few hours, though Taniel tried to remind himself that the northern half of the city was still generally intact.

Taniel and Ka-poel rowed across the river to where a familiar figure waited for them on the far bank.

Styke wore his faded yellow cavalry jacket and pants and

stood without a hat, the rain trickling down his face. His jaw was black and blue from where the Warden had struck him but he seemed otherwise whole, pulling their canoe onto the bank with one hand.

"She was a tough woman," Styke said. "Pit of a thing, leading an untrained garrison into the teeth of the damned like that."

After you, you big bloody fool. Taniel almost spat the words out loud, a war of emotion going through his head. He wanted to punch Styke square in the face—which, after what he'd seen him do to the Warden, seemed like a bad idea—but he also knew deep down that if they'd hunkered down Planth, they would have lost the city. Styke's mad charge had saved them all. Bertreau's sacrifice had saved them all.

Taniel bit down on his tongue for several moments before nodding. "Have we heard from the Kez yet?"

"They want to talk," Styke said.

He and Styke, accompanied by a few dozen Mad Lancers decked out in their armor, met the Kez delegation in approximately the same spot they'd met General Jiffou five afternoons ago. Taniel's group arrived first and watched the others approach at a distance.

"They look more wet and miserable than I feel," Taniel said.

Styke snorted. "The storm will have softened them up. They camped too close to the river and half a dozen of their supply wagons floated away last night. They've no way to dry their clothes, tents, or powder."

"You've had them watched?" Taniel asked, shooting Styke a sharp glance.

"Closely. Also been taking counts. That battle cost them four casualties for every one of ours, and word has it infection is going rampant among their wounded."

Taniel shook his head. He shouldn't be surprised to find Styke attentive enough to spy on the Kez. He was, after all, a decorated colonel. But the single-mindedness of his fighting spirit made it hard to see anything else but the Mad Lancer.

The Kez delegation came to a stop a dozen yards away. "They look…" Taniel said, "younger."

"That's Major Bahr," Styke responded. "Thanks to you, he's the highest-ranking officer in their brigade right now."

Major Bahr couldn't have been older than thirty. He was a stout man, the buttons of his jacket a little tight around his waist, but he handled his horse comfortably as he closed the gap between them. He looked over his shoulder once then cleared his throat.

"Colonel Styke," he said.

"Major Bahr. Pleased to meet you. Have you come to offer your surrender?"

The joke seemed entirely out of place, but to be honest, Taniel wasn't sure it *was* a joke.

"I've come to ask for the surrender of the city."

"You think we'll hand over the city after the thrashing we gave you the other day?" Taniel asked.

"Using our own bugle signals to force a retreat was inspired, to be sure, but it hardly constitutes a thrashing. You have nothing left—half a thousand men at best, and no artillery. If I press, the city will fall."

"If you press," Taniel said, "I will put a bullet between your eyes. You won't even see if coming." His father had always told him that the threat of a powder mage to the enemy officers should be silent and implied, or it would lose its potency. Taniel had heard his father break his own rule on more than one occasion and thought this was just as good of a spot to do so again.

Styke's warhorse danced beneath him, and Styke added, "Once he's done that, I'll ride my lancers up and down your ranks until I trample every last one of you into the mud."

"Lindet is long gone," Taniel said. "The city is a ruin and half the people have left. There's nothing here for you but bugs, snakes, and malevolence. Turn around, and the Tristan Ghost Irregulars will leave you alone until you're well out of the Basin. I give you my word."

Bahr cleared his throat a second time, looking between Styke and Taniel, before he finally settled his gaze somewhere in between. "Our intelligence confirms that Lindet fled almost a week ago. Our officer corps has been all but destroyed, and I am not willing to advance without replacements. I give you notice that the brigade intends to withdraw tomorrow morning and I hope you'll stick to your promise of an unmolested retreat. Good day, sirs."

Taniel watched the Kez delegation return to their camp. Despite the horror of the last few days, he felt a sudden lightness in his chest.

"We won," he breathed.

Styke chuckled. "Chubby bastard just tried to bluff us. Good for him." He looked up into the sky. "Rain's clearing up."

"We won," Taniel repeated. "We didn't just buy time. We saved the city." He could hardly believe it. The mad charge, the loss of half the garrison, even Bertreau's death—it hadn't been for nothing.

Styke leaned over and slapped him on the shoulder, almost knocking him off his horse. "Well done, Two-shot. You saved a lot of lives."

"So did you."

Styke shrugged. "I just ride."

Taniel wondered how much Styke was deferring credit, and how much he truly had led the charge out of something else—a lust for glory, a suicidal touch, or just a deep-set madness. Styke himself might not know.

Taniel frowned, looking over his shoulder at the ruins of Planth. Styke followed his gaze and must have sensed something of what he was thinking because he said, "I've seen dead cities before, with the land salted and the foundations destroyed. Planth is not that. It's a crossroads. The people will return and rebuild."

There was an optimism in his tone that made Taniel smile, and he knew that Lindet was not wholly right about Styke. Styke cared. He'd see that these people survived.

The wind was changing. The sky, as Styke had said, began to clear. Taniel knew the Fatrastan revolution was not over, but he had the feeling his time in the Basin was coming to a close. The Ghost Irregulars would need a new commander, new orders, and he himself might need to move on before too long.

For the first time in months, he truly longed for home.

For more in the Powder Mage Universe:

Promise of Blood
The Powder Mage Trilogy
Orbit, April 2013

The Crimson Campaign
The Powder Mage Trilogy
Orbit, May 2014

The Autumn Republic
The Powder Mage Trilogy
Orbit, February 2015

Forsworn
A Powder Mage Novella
January 2014

Servant of the Crown
A Powder Mage Novella
June 2014

Murder at the Kinnen Hotel
A Powder Mage Novella
November 2014

In the Field Marshal's Shadow
Stories from the Powder Mage Universe
November 2015

Acknowledgements

Rene Aigner - cover artist
Michele McClellan - editor
Jillena O'Brien - copy editor
Michele McClellan - map artist

Special Thanks to Bob Case, Dale Triplett, Danielle Bordelon, Fergus McCartan, Gabe Mielke, James Cox, Jason McDonald, Justin Heard, Kamden Blackstone, Kristina Pick, Mark Lindberg, Matt Thyer, Peter Keep, Robert Holland, Ryan Faulk, and Samuel Grawe.

Contact Brian McClellan

brian@brianmcclellan.com

GHOSTS OF THE
TRISTAN BASIN